Praise for *The Black Ice S*

T0084793

"Parker ultimately scores again in this lean and hungry tale."

Allen J. Hubin, *New York Times Book Review*

"Richard Stark's Parker . . . is refreshingly amoral, a thief who always gets away with the swag."

Stephen King, *Entertainment Weekly*

"Richard Stark's Parker novels . . . are among the most poised and polished fictions of their time and, in fact, of any time."

John Banville, *Bookforum*

"You can read the entire series and not once have to invest in a bookmark."

Luc Sante

"It's excellent to have [Stark's novels] readily available again—not so much masterpieces of genre, just master-pieces, period."

Richard Rayner, *L. A. Times*

"The caper novel, the story of a major criminal operation from the point of view of the participants, has no better practitioner than Richard Stark."

Anthony Boucher, *New York Times Book Review*

"One of the most original characters in mystery fiction has returned without a loss of step, savvy, sheer bravado, street smarts, or sense of survival."

Mystery News

The Black Ice Score

Parker Novels By Richard Stark

The Black Ice Score

RICHARD STARK

With a New Foreword by Dennis Lehane

The University of Chicago Press

The University of Chicago Press, Chicago, 60637
Copyright © 1965 by Donald Westlake
Foreword © 2010 by Dennis Lehane
All rights reserved.
University of Chicago Press edition 2010

Printed in the United States of America

19 18 17 16 15 14 13 12 11   2 3 4 5

ISBN-13: 978-0-226-77109-0 (paper)
ISBN-10: 0-226-77109-1 (paper

Library of Congress Cataloging-in-Publication Data

Stark, Richard, 1933–2008.
  The black ice score : a Parker novel / Richard Stark ; with a new foreword by
Dennis Lehane.
     p. cm.
  Originally published: London : Fawcett, 1967.
  Summary: Emissaries from a small African nation ask Parker to help them
steal back half of their country's wealth in diamonds.
  ISBN-13: 978-0-226-77109-0 (pbk. : alk. paper)
  ISBN-10: 0-226-77109-1 (pbk. : alk. paper) 1. Parker (Fictitious
character)—Fiction. 2. Criminals—Fiction. I. Title.
  PS3573.E9B56 2010
  813'.54—dc22
                            2009039264

⊛ The paper used in this publication meets the minimum requirements of the
American National Standard for Information Sciences—Permanence of Paper
for Printed Library Materials, ANSI Z39.48-1992.

I had drinks with Donald Westlake once at a crime fiction conference in the winter of 2000. We talked mostly about two terrific scripts he wrote in the late eighties, one for Stephen Frears (*The Grifters*), the other for Joseph Ruben (*The Stepfather*), but we never discussed his alter ego Richard Stark or Stark's indelible creation, Parker. This would be less surprising if I weren't such a geek about the Parker books. I'd read them all in the summer of '86, (there were sixteen at that point.) Along with Elmore Leonard's work, they taught me nearly everything I know about how to execute violence on the page. As for Parker himself, he's a watershed character in American noir, nearly incomparable. So why didn't I fly my geek flag while hanging with the man who created him?

A sense of mystery, for one; I don't want to know too much about the artists who create the art that excites me. The collective dream that descends upon the reader of a fictional universe depends on believing that the dream is quite real, even while you know, of course, that it's not. I feared the more I learned about the mechanical strings behind Parker the more artificial he would seem. And finally, the writer is about the last person you should trust when it comes to interpreting his work. If we truly knew what we were doing, we probably wouldn't do it; it would feel too much like a straight job.

As to Westlake, himself, he matched my preconceived impression of the creator of the John Dortmunder novels—a wry, intelligent man, self-deprecating and steeped in irony. Such was Donald Westlake. Richard Stark, however, was nowhere to be found. Because as playful as Donald Westlake is, Richard Stark is all business. Where Westlake's writing is chummy, Stark's is clinical. If Westlake is the guy you'd love to find sitting beside you at the bar on a raw March night, Stark is the guy you'd hope to avoid in the parking lot on your way home.

As a stylist, Richard Stark's sense of economy is surgical. He has no time for flatulent prose; one senses he holds the decorous in contempt. He evokes a world of medium-sized, nondescript cities or dusty flatlands. A lot of the action takes place in motel rooms, either the kind with wrought iron fire escapes right out the window or those "with concrete block walls painted green, the imitation Danish modern furniture, the rough beige carpeting, not enough towels." Like those motel rooms and like Parker, Stark is a model of efficiency. This isn't to say his style lacks amenities. The swift sentences move with a running back's fluid timing. He could no more be accused of soulless functionality than could Hemingway or Raymond Carver. Stark writes with economy, yes, and cold, cold clarity, but there's grace in the prose, a stripped-bare poetry made all the more admirable for its lack of self-consciousness.

And what did that cold clarity produce?

Parker. The greatest antihero in American noir. If Parker ever had a heart, he left it behind in a drawer one morning and never came back for it. He never cracks a joke, inquires about someone's health or family, feels regret or shame or even rage. And not once in the sixteen novels that comprise the FPE (First Parker Epoch, 1962–74) does he wink at the reader. You know the Wink. It's what the "supposedly" amoral character does to let the reader know he's not *really* as bad as he seems. Maybe, in fact, he's been the good guy all along.

Parker *is* as bad as he seems. If a baby carriage rolled in front of him during a heist, he'd kick it out of his way. If an innocent woman were caught helplessly in gangster cross-fire, Parker would slip past her, happy she was drawing the bullets away from him. If you hit him, he'd hit you back twice as hard. If you stole from him, he'd burn your house—or corporation—to the ground to get his money back. And if, as in *Butcher's Moon*, the sixteenth of the sixteen FPE novels, you were stupid enough to kidnap one of his guys and hold him hostage in a safe house, he would kill every single one of you. He'd shoot you through a door, shoot you in the face, shoot you in the back and step over your body before it stopped twitching.

Nothing personal, by the way. He gets no pleasure from the shooting or the twitching. He's not a psychopath, after all, he's a sociopath. But first and foremost, he is a professional. He's the progenitor of many a fictional criminal antihero, but those progeny are always redeemed by a need to connect with the human race. James Ellroy's antiheroes come immediately to mind, and it's hard to think of a more resolutely scumbag act than the protagonist of *White Jazz* throwing a mentally handicapped man out a window in chapter one. Yet by chapter thirty, he's reached out to the reader along the lines of shared humanity, and he's garnered our empathy, if not our love. Similarly, in the films of Michael Mann, many of the protagonists, from Frank in *Thief* to Dillinger in *Public Enemies*, share Parker's emotional retardation and consummate professionalism, but in that very professionalism Mann finds nobility. Cop Vincent Hanna in *Heat* clearly admires the work ethic of criminal Neil McCauley, while Frank in *Thief* asks the cops who shake him down why they don't try, as he does, to actually work for a living. But in the moral universe of the Parker novels, the very idea of nobility is laughable—Parker *is* a sociopath. The world he inhabits, however, is worse.

It's a world of absolute rot. Nothing and no one is above it and most are happiest that way. The Outfit sits atop a pyramid comprised of luckless thugs, idiot muscle, hustlers, grifters, hookers with hearts of bile, and bloody avarice so banal yet so all-encompassing as to wallpaper every room in every scene of every one of the sixteen Parker novels. The

Outfit casts its shadows everywhere. It's the grimy engine that runs the grimy car with the faulty brakes and the crap transmission, yet when the brakes blow and the transmission seizes, the Outfit tells you it's your fault. And your bill.

Who can fight against this? Not the hero with the heart of gold. Not the Nice Guy or the Good Guy or the Morally Compromised But Ultimately Nice Good Guy. No. Only a cog in the machine can screw up the machine. A piece of the machine as grimy and hard as the rest of it. A chunk of steel. Or pipe of lead.

Parker is the lead pipe. He has no illusions about the machine—not a single ideal left to shred or a romantic notion left to dispel. Like the machine, he is heartless. And this is where he differs from every other antihero in noir. James Ellroy's protagonists have heart, however deeply buried. Jim Thompson's characters might not have heart or sentimental notions, but they are ultimately punished for that lack. Same goes for James M. Cain's lecherous ids-run-amok. Hammett gave us Sam Spade, he of the physical resemblance to the devil, who finds his partner's killer not out of noble principle but solely because it would be bad business not to. But while Spade may have no feelings for Archer, he is in love with Brigid O'Shaughnessy. Again, humanity creeps in whether the protagonist wants it to or not. This is a foundation brick of literary narrative—the antihero discovers his humanity, which allows us, the readers, to recognize ourselves in him and feel communion with the human race as a whole.

To which Parker says, screw that. Parker refuses to reveal his heart. Parker authentically and resolutely eschews sentiment. Or emotion. Parker never asks for understanding or grasps for a common cord between himself and the reader. (If the common cord held monetary value, he'd steal it. Otherwise, it's all yours.) What Parker represents, at least to me, is the abolition of the wish fulfillment that forms the firmament of narrative literature, a firmament I, myself, usually require, both as a reader and a writer. The wishes being fulfilled are familiar—good wins out, love conquers all, crime never pays, the check is in the mail. Well, in this case, the check *was* in the mail, but Parker intercepted it. And cashed it. And used it to finance a crime that paid double what you'll make this year.

So why do we like him for it? Why do we root for him? Why is it, after reading sixteen novels depicting the adventures of a heartless sociopath in the summer of '86, did I feel the desire for more? Why do I still look back on these novels, as a reader, with great affection and, as a writer, with wonder?

I still don't know the answer. Not absolutely. I *suspect*. I suspect we all recognize the Lie, even as we wrap our arms around it and hug it tight to keep us warm. The Lie is the illusion that we are safe, that we are watched over, that we will go gently and that the night is good. Not so, says Richard Stark. Not so, says Parker.

We are not safe. No one is looking out for us. And the night? The night is dark. So let's get to work before the sun comes up. Before someone catches us at it. Before the world wakes up.

Dennis Lehane

The Black Ice Score

One

.

1

Parker walked into his hotel room, and there was a guy in there going through his suitcase laid out on his bed. He looked over when Parker came in and calmly said, "That'll be all right." He had some kind of accent.

And he hadn't been talking to Parker. Parker looked behind himself, and number two was shutting the door. Number three was to the left, over by the window; he was the only one with hardware showing, an automatic held negligently in his right hand pointed nowhere in particular.

The faces were all strangers. They were all about forty, tall, in good physical condition, well dressed, deeply tanned. They might be law, but they didn't smell like it. They smelled like something new, something Parker didn't know anything about.

He said, "Where's the woman?" because Claire was supposed to be in here; she was here when he'd gone out, and he didn't like the idea of her being around guns.

The one at the suitcase nodded his head toward the closed bathroom door. "In there," he said. "On a promise of good behavior."

Number two, standing directly behind Parker, said, "Hold your arms out from your sides, please." He had the same sort of accent as the first one, and the "please" was a surprise. Like some levels of law, maybe federal. But not with the accents. And not with the feel of them, the general manner.

Parker put his hands out to his sides, and number two patted him up and down. It was a thorough frisk but not a professional one. He took too long to cover the territory, as though he wasn't sure of his ability to get it right.

When the patting was done, number two said, "Right." Parker put his arms down again.

"If you don't mind," number one said, "I'll just finish up here."

Parker looked at number three's gun. He didn't say anything.

Number one didn't wait for an answer. He kept on poking through Parker's suitcase, not being unnecessarily sloppy but not trying to be too careful either. Most of the drawers in the room were partly open, so the suitcase was the last thing to be searched.

What were they looking for? Parker had no idea, so he stood in the middle of the room and waited to find out who they were and what they wanted and what his best move was. Number one poked at his gear in the suitcase, number two stood with his back against the hall door, and number three leaned against the wall near the window, the automatic in his hand filling the room with a silent buzz. Outside the window and seven stories down, the New York City traffic inched along making muffled noises. The sky out there was gray, mid-March gray. Wherever these three had picked up their tans, it wasn't in New York.

Parker looked at the closed bathroom door. What shape was Claire in? Violence shook her up, even the hint of violence; it reminded her of a time she didn't want to think about. If they'd leaned on her she was probably having silent hysterics in there now. She could do anything, react in a million different ways. She might come screaming out with a pair of nail scissors in her fist; it was impossible to say.

Parker said, "Let me talk to my woman while you're doing that."

"Just finishing up." He turned away from the suitcase, leaving it open on the bed, and gave Parker a wintry smile. "She hasn't been hurt, I assure you," he said. "Not so far, at any rate."

Parker felt his shoulder muscles tensing. He wanted to

8

move out of this, switch the odds on this trio, find out what they thought they were doing. The only sensible thing to do was wait, but that was the thing he was bad at.

Number one said, "You can sit down, if you like, while we talk."

"I'll stand."

"Suit yourself." He sat on the foot of Claire's bed. He produced a pack of cigarettes. "Smoke?"

"No."

He shrugged and lit a cigarette for himself, then took it from his mouth and looked at it. "Overrated, American cigarettes," he said. "Though I suppose it's what one grows used to."

"Do you have something you want to get to?" Parker asked him.

He raised an eyebrow. He seemed to be trying for the studied British effect, but it didn't quite work. There was farmer in him somewhere, farmer or cattleman, something like that. He said, "I think you can guess, Mr Parker, what we're here for."

Parker didn't like that. He was here under his other name, Matthew Walker, the name he used when he wasn't working. He didn't like it that these people knew so much about him and he knew nothing about them. He said, "I don't make guesses. You're here, you're going through my goods, you're making muscles. I don't know why. Right now you're having fun, taking your time. Later on you'll tell me."

Number three, over by the window, said, "A very hard case, this one." He seemed amused.

Number one shook his head. He said to Parker, "Very well, you're a cautious man. So I'll make things plain for you. We're here to talk to you about your current project."

"I have no current project," Parker told him. It was the truth, but he didn't expect these three to believe it.

They didn't. Number one smiled and shook his head. "There's no point in any of this," he said. "We know

9

everything about you. Your name is Parker, you travel with a woman named Claire — the young lady now in the bathroom — and you are a professional thief. Your specialty is planning the details of large-scale robberies."

That was all true. Parker said nothing.

Number one waited, looking at Parker, asking for a response. Finally he said, "You don't deny it? Don't admit it? Nothing?"

"Get to the point," Parker said.

"That *is* the point," he said. "You have been approached on a certain project. There's no need to go into details, for God's sake." He was suddenly nettled, as though Parker were delaying him in some important series of events.

"Go into details," Parker said.

"No. How do I know how much or how little they've told you?"

"Who?"

"This is very foolish."

Number three said, "The point is, are you going in with them?"

Parker turned his head and looked at him. "Going in with who?"

Number three smiled sardonically at number one. "I think he is," he said. "That's why he's carrying on like this; he's already committed himself to the other side."

"Perhaps," said number one. "Or perhaps he's merely undecided." He looked at Parker. "I'm going to assume that's the case," he said. "And I'm going to suggest to you that you not get involved."

Parker said, "In what?"

"Don't waste my time!"

Number two, at the door behind Parker, said, "Two or three lost teeth would be the best convincer."

Number one shook his head. "Only if it's absolutely necessary," he said. To Parker he said, "Ostensibly, you and your lady friend are here from Miami on a shopping trip.

10

Content yourself with that. *Make* it a shopping trip. And bring it soon to a conclusion, and return to Miami. Do not get involved. If you don't already know the caliber of the people who've approached you, allow me to tell you they are useless. Worse than useless. Liabilities. You know the kind they are, you seem to be a sensible man. You aren't simply bucking the Colonel's stooges, you're bucking *us*. I don't think you'll want to do that."

Parker said, "If I ever find out what you're talking about, I'll bear what you said in mind."

"Cautious to the end, eh?" He smiled and got to his feet, flicking cigarette ash on the rug. "Very well, then," he said. "We'll leave it at that. For the moment."

They trooped to the door. Parker turned and looked at them, the three of them standing together, looking like cousins, threads of similarity among them, that touch of the farmer in all three of them.

Number one paused, his hand on the knob. "I hope," he said, "for your sake, we never have to meet again."

Parker said nothing.

Number one waited, expecting a response, then shrugged and opened the door and went out. The other two followed.

2

Claire was sitting on the closed toilet lid, knees together, arms hugging herself. She was a good-looking woman, a stylish woman, but fear had made her angular and jagged and old.

Parker stayed in the doorway, his hand on the knob. "They're gone," he said.

She thawed slowly, straightening, her arms losing their tension, her face relaxing back toward something he recognized. She said, "Who—" and stopped because her voice was rusty. She coughed and cleared her throat, ducking her head in a gesture he knew, and looked up at him to say, "Who were they? What did they want?"

"They didn't say."

"You can tell me," she said. "This time, you can tell me."

He knew she meant the agreement they had that he wouldn't ever talk to her about the life he had when he was being Parker. He shook his head. "They didn't say. They were full of something I don't know about, and they wouldn't believe I wasn't in on it."

She stood up, moving slowly as though she were stiff, holding on to the sink for support. "What did they want?"

"To tell me not to get involved."

"In what?"

"They didn't say."

She frowned at him, frustrated, then suddenly grinned as though something unexpected had struck her funny. "Really?" she said.

He nodded. "Really."

"They came in and acted tough and told you not to get

involved and they wouldn't say in what?" She was grinning broadly now.

"Don't get hysterical," he said.

"I'm not going to get hysterical. I was afraid of them, really afraid of them, and they're just . . . silly. Just silly men."

"Maybe," Parker said.

"I think I'll come out of the bathroom now," she said, and her smile was more natural, as though maybe she wouldn't have hysterics.

"Fine," he said. He put his hand out toward her and she took it, holding tight.

She came out to the main room and looked around. "They searched," she said.

"Yes."

"I don't suppose you know for what."

"No."

She looked at him, and though she was still smiling her eyes were a little shadowed. "Shall we drink in the room," she said, "or go out?"

"Here."

"Good. I'll call."

She let his hand go and walked between the beds to the stand with the phone, but just as she got to it it rang. She stopped, hand partway out toward the phone, and looked back at Parker to say, "Am I stupid? I want you to answer it."

"That's not stupid," Parker said. The phone rang again as he went by her. He picked up the receiver, said, "Yes?"

"Mr Walker?" The voice insinuated; it was made of oil.

"Yes," Parker said.

"Have they left?"

Parker stiffened. Out of the corner of his eye he could see Claire watching him, saw her react to his reaction. He said, "Yes."

"I hope they were not . . . too much trouble."

"No," Parker said. Claire was watching him as though to read the other half of the conversation on his forehead.

"Did you make a decision?" the voice asked.

"Not yet," he said.

"Then there might be some profit in our having a talk?"

"I don't know. Who are you?"

"Oh, you don't know me, Mr Walker. But let's say I was in your shoes once, that I might be able to offer you the benefit of my experience. Would you be interested?"

"Yes," Parker said.

"Then may I sug—" *Click.*

The line was dead.

Parker said, "Hello?"

Claire said, "What is it?"

Parker shook his head. He put the receiver back on its cradle and said, "I don't like this."

"What was it?"

"Another one. He wanted to know if they'd left, wanted to know if I'd like to have a talk with him. Then the connection got broken."

"What are we going to do?"

He looked at her. "Nothing," he said. "If somebody else shows up, I'll try to find out what's going on. If not, we forget it."

"Can you? That easily?"

"Why not?"

She spread her hands. "I don't know. Curiosity, something. Sometimes you don't seem—" She shrugged and turned away. "I don't think I want that drink after all," she said.

"What do you want instead?"

"Do you think we should go back? Back to Miami?"

"No."

She looked at him. "Why not?"

He didn't tell her the reason. The reason was they were only at this hotel in New York for a few days, so if trouble happened here it couldn't louse up much. But in Miami they were known, they had a pattern developed; if there was

14

trouble down there it could spoil a lot of things. But to talk to her about trouble would only make her nervous, so he said, "Because we're here to shop. Some people got their wires crossed, but they'll find out it was a mistake and that's the end of it. They didn't tell me enough to make me dangerous to them, and after a while they'll find out I'm not in on their thing,'whatever it is, so they won't be back."

She looked dubious. "Are you sure?"

"I'm not packing," he said.

She looked at the open suitcase on the bed. "You think it's safe to stay here?"

"Yes. And I think you ought to go out. Go to some stores, buy some things. That's what you're here for. It'll get those three out of your head."

"You won't come with me?"

"I'll cramp your style," he told her. "Go on and buy things."

"I don't like this!" she said, suddenly bursting it out.

Parker went over and put his hands on her arms. "They didn't hurt you," he said. "They leaned a little and said don't get involved. So we're not getting involved, so it's all over. I know this kind of thing; you can take my word for it."

She looked at him, and he could see her wanting to believe him. "Can I really?"

"You can."

She began to shiver. He pulled her in and held her, and the shivering settled down, and after a while she nodded against his jaw and said, "I'm all right."

He let her go. "You want a drink now?"

"No I will go shopping. That's what I was going to do this afternoon, so why not?"

"That's right," he said.

It took her five minutes to get ready. He sat on the bed and watched her, pleased by her existence but in a hurry for her to be gone, and when she'd kissed him and left he picked up the phone and called a number in uptown Manhattan

15

and asked to speak to Fred.

"Speaking."

"This is Colt," Parker said. "I need a traveling iron. Can I get one delivered to the hotel?"

"Are you a referral, Mr Colt?"

"A friend of mine named Parker recommended you."

"Oh, yes. Mr Parker, I remember him. Did you have any special kind of iron in mind, Mr Colt?"

"What do you have available?"

"Oh, most kinds. The thirty-two-dollar circular model, or the larger one at thirty-eight dollars. Or the forty-five-dollar automatic steam model. Then there are some nice German irons."

"The thirty-two-dollar model's good enough," Parker said.

"Excellent. And you want that delivered?"

"Yes. Normanton Hotel, West Forty-sixth Street, room seven twenty-three."

"And that will be cash on delivery."

"Naturally," said Parker. "How soon can it get here?"

"Is this a rush order?"

"Yes."

"Hmmmm." There was a silence, and then: "Within the hour."

"Fine," Parker said, and hung up.

Fifty minutes later there was a knock at the door. Parker opened and let in a messenger with a package. "Fifty bucks," the messenger said.

Parker paid him, in cash, and he left. Parker opened the package and took out a Smith and Wesson Terrier .32-caliber revolver, a stubby five-shot pistol with a two-inch barrel. There was also a box of cartridges in the package. Parker loaded the revolver and tucked it away under the pillow of his bed.

16

3

Claire said, "You have no more money."

Parker, sitting on the bed, his back against the pillow, looked at her and saw she was over it. She'd believed his assurances, and the shopping had taken her mind off it more, and the raw, windy day outside had given her good color. She looked fine, happy and healthy, dropping packages on the other bed. She'd come in with a double armload of boxes and bags.

Parker said, "Let's see."

"One at a time," she said. "I'll give you a fashion show."

"Good."

She rummaged among the packages, selected two and went into the bathroom, leaving the door open. Calling out to him, she said, "The crowds were incredible. I'd forgotten."

He listened to her, but didn't have the attention to find anything to answer. He was thinking about the three this morning, and the other one on the phone, and when they'd come back, and what their attitude would be this time.

From the bathroom Claire called, "And do you think you can find anything in the color you want? Not a bit of it."

Should he send Claire back to Miami by herself? But then if nothing else happened the trip would be spoiled for no reason.

"But it's worth it," she called, and came out of the bathroom smiling, wearing plum and gold. Holding her arms out, she turned in a slow circle. "Isn't it?" she said.

Parker looked at her, and again he was pleased to have her to look at. "You look good," he said.

"That's the whole point," she said, and the phone rang.

She stopped in the middle of a pirouette, one arm awkwardly curved. She looked at the phone.

Parker picked it up. "Yes?"

"I'm sorry we were cut off before. It was unavoidable. They very nearly saw me."

It was the same oily voice. Parker said, "You were down in the lobby?"

"Yes, of course. It was necessary for me to leave and then follow them again till they lit. But I'm back now."

"Downstairs?"

Claire shook her head, as though to deny it was happening.

"Shall I come up?"

"I'll come down," Parker said. "I'll meet you in the bar."

"A public place might not be the best."

"You're not coming up here," Parker said.

The voice sighed. "Very well. You will find me wearing a red tie. I do not know what you look like, so it will be necessary for you to come to me."

"All right. I'll be down in five minutes."

"Very good."

Parker hung up and got to his feet. Claire said, "The man who called before?"

"Yes. I'm going down and talk to him." He took the pistol out from under his pillow and tucked it into his left hip pcket.

Her eyes widened when she saw the gun. "You didn't have that before."

"I'll be back in a little while," he said. "Put the night lock on. Don't open the door to anybody but me."

"You knew it wasn't done with," she said, staring at him. "You knew they'd be back."

"It was a chance. I won't be long." He put on his jacket and left.

4

The hotel bar was a dark, square room with the bar along the back wall and the rest of the space taken up with low tables flanked by low, broad Naugahyde chairs, everything in shades of brown with brass fixtures. Parker sat at the first table to the right, just inside the door. There was a bowl of peanuts there. He took a handful of peanuts, ate a couple, and looked at the reflection in the back bar mirror of the man with the red necktie sitting at the end of the bar.

Perhaps thirty. Suit a little bit seedy but proper, a nondescript brown. Face handsome but weak, with a yellow-tan moustache, as though his dreams of glory included being a British air ace of the First World War. His hair was yellow-tan, too, and thinning, the long hairs brushed straight back from a slightly flushed forehead. He was drinking something with a cherry and a slice of orange in it, and he betrayed nervousness only by constantly looking at himself in the mirror and constantly turning and turning his glass on the bar.

There were about a dozen other customers in the bar. Parker watched them all, and when he was sure none of them cared about the man with the red necktie he shook his head at the waiter finally coming this way, got to his feet, and walked over to sit at the bar.

The other looked at him in the back bar mirror. His lips curved into a little V of a smile under his moustache, like a pornographer about to show his pictures, and he murmured, "Mr Walker. A pleasure."

"I didn't get your name." Parker didn't bother with the

19

mirror routine. He turned his head and watched the other's profile, less than arm's reach away. All around, people murmured their conversations together.

"Hoskins." He kept looking at the mirror, and bowed to it. "How do you do?"

"What do you want, Hoskins?"

"So very direct." Still with that little smile, Hoskins shook his head at the mirror and sipped at his drink. Putting the glass down he said, "We shouldn't rush into this, Mr Walker, not till we know each other a little better."

Parker controlled his impatience. If Claire hadn't been around on this trip, he would have agreed to meet Hoskins in the room, and by now Hoskins would be talking very fast, in complete and informative sentences. But the way things were there was no place private to take Hoskins, and in public here there was no way to hurry him.

He turned away from Hoskins to the bartender passing by. "Scotch and water."

"Sir."

He looked back at Hoskins. "It's your ball," he said.

Hoskins ducked his head slightly, still smiling, as though he'd been complimented and was showing a pretty embarrassment. Then he turned his head to look at Parker directly, his little smile disappeared, and he said, "What did you tell them?"

"That I didn't know what was going on."

Hoskins made an impatient gesture. "Not *them*," he said. "Gonor and that bunch of his, what did you tell them?"

Parker said, "Why?"

The little smile came back. "I have to know if you're working for them, don't I? I have to know if your sense of loyalty is involved, don't I?"

"It isn't," Parker said.

"You told them no?"

"I haven't told them anything."

Hoskins was pleased. "Good," he said. "Let him wait a

little while, let him get anxious. That was my mistake, you know; I looked too eager, I jumped too soon. I admit it, I was too anxious."

"So now you're out?"

Hoskins looked surprised. "They wouldn't be coming to you if I was still their man, would they?"

"No, they wouldn't," said Parker. He was still waiting for Hoskins to say the one thing that would turn all the rest of this gibberish into sense. Given enough time, and by the obvious slackness of his nature, Hoskins finally would come up with it. All it took was patience, which for Parker did not come naturally.

"There's plenty in it for two men," Hoskins was saying.

"They tell you how much?"

"No."

Hoskins nodded grimly. "Full of little hints, aren't they? But they won't come right out with it. Well, I tell you I'm convinced it can't be less than a million! It can't be! It only stands to reason. The Colonel wouldn't walk out with less than that, would he?"

"Maybe not," Parker said. He was wondering if the Colonel was the same as Gonor, the other name Hoskins had mentioned. Or was the Colonel one of the three who'd been in the room before?

Hoskins said, "So there's plenty for two men, you can see that. Two smart men working together. *White* men. You see what I mean." .

"It's possible," Parker said, and the bartender appeared and put his drink in front of him, saying:

"Are you Mr Walker?"

"Yes."

"You're wanted on the phone, sir. I'll bring it to you."

The bartender went away, and Hoskins, looking very suspicious and nervous, said, "Is that them?"

"My wife is the only one who knows I'm here," Parker said. He and Claire were traveling as Mr and Mrs Walker,

21

and since this one obviously didn't know about the Parker name, he probably accepted Claire's wife status, too. In any case, it was simplest to describe her that way.

Hoskins worked moodily at his drink while they waited for the phone to be brought. He didn't look at Parker at all now, neither directly nor in the mirror, but gloomily studied the surface of the bar as though thinking about flaws in his course of action.

The bartender brought the phone and handed the receiver to Parker.

Parker said, "Yes?"

It was Claire. "There are four men here," she said. It was hard to tell anything from her voice.

Parker said, "The same?"

"No," she said. "These are different ones. I told them about the others, and what you're doing now, and they promised to explain everything."

"Why did you?"

"Tell them? They aren't like the others; you'll see. There's nothing to worry about."

There was always something to worry about when various groups were maneuvering around each other and at least one of them was flashing guns, but Parker didn't say anything about that. He said, "I'll be right up," and hung up.

Hoskins was watching him worriedly. "Trouble?"

"My wife wants to see me. I have to go up for just a minute. You want to come along or wait here?"

"I believe I'll wait," Hoskins said.

"Watch my drink," Parker told him. "I'll be right back."

5

Four black men in red robes stood and sat around the room, like a scene in a Negro version of *Julius Caesar*. Claire, legs crossed, cigarette in hand, at ease, sat in the chair near the window. She was still wearing the new outfit she'd put on to show him just before he left.

Parker shut the door with his left hand and let the hand dangle near his hip. He looked around at the faces.

Claire made the introductions, gesturing at the one of the four who was coming toward Parker now with a solemn face and an outstretched hand. "Mr Gonor," she said, "this is Mr Parker. Parker, this is Gonor."

The use of the name surprised him. He looked away from Gonor at Claire.

She smiled slightly and shook her head. "That was the name they knew," she said. "Like the other ones."

"We are most sorry about that experience," Gonor said. His hand was still out. He was short, no more than five feet tall, and he looked up solemnly at Parker as he spoke. "They got to you before we did," he said. He had some sort of faint accent too, a little harsher than the first group. It might have been two versions of the same accent, such as German might be if spoken by an American from the North and an American from the South.

Parker said, "Is that what it was? They thought I'd already talked to you so I'd already know what was going on?"

"Yes." Gonor's hand was still out there, undaunted.

"And the same with Hoskins," Parker said.

Gonor's hand dropped to his side, and his expression became suddenly wary. "Hoskins? You know him?"

"I just met him. He called me and we met and talked. He thought I knew about things too. He's downstairs now, waiting for me. In the bar."

Gonor turned his head and said something short and harsh in a language Parker had never heard before. Two of the others nodded and headed for the door.

Parker put his back against the door. "I haven't taken sides yet," he said. "The advertisement was you were going to tell me what's going on."

"What did Hoskins tell you?"

"Nothing. Doubletalk, like the other bunch."

"He shouldn't be here," Gonor said. "He shouldn't be involved any more; he was told to stay away."

"He'll keep," Parker said. "Tell me the story first."

Gonor cocked his head to one side. "Have you made a deal with him? Is that why you don't want us to go get him?"

"Get him and do what with him?"

"Bring him up here. Make sure he stays away from now on."

Parker moved away from the door. "Bring him up," he said. "That's a good idea. If you see the other bunch, bring them up too. Let's find out what's going on."

"You'll find out, Mr Parker."

The other two were heading for the door again. Parker said to them, "Hoskins only knows me as Walker."

"It isn't our intention to endanger the structure of your life, Mr Parker," Gonor said. "We'll use the Walker name, if you prefer."

"I prefer."

The two went out, and Gonor said, "First, I suppose I should present my credentials. I have been sent to you by a Mr McKay, who operates a restaurant in a small city in Maine."

"A diner," Parker said.

Gonor nodded. "Yes. A small restaurant, with chrome."

"All right," Parker said. Handy McKay was the one man

24

who knew Parker's whereabouts and what name he was living under. Anybody who wanted to get in touch with Parker had to do so through Handy.

Gonor said, "We were sent to Mr McKay, in turn, by a man named Karns. Do you also know him?"

"Yes," Parker said. A few years ago he'd had some trouble with a gambling-and-narcotics syndicate, and he'd had to get rid of the man at the top of it. Karns had taken that man's place and had been grateful to Parker for making it possible.

"We went to Mr Karns," Gonor said, "when Hoskins failed to be what we had in mind. We were looking for a criminal, but of a very particular kind. Hoskins is certainly a criminal, but not with the qualifications we need."

"Karns didn't send you to Hoskins?"

"No. We found Hoskins on our own." Gonor shook his head, as though reflecting on great difficulties in the past. "The United States is a large and complex nation," he said. "A nation of specialists. Here more than anywhere else in the world there will be someone capable of handling any specific task, no matter how unusual. The only problem is to find him."

Claire said, "Mr Gonor, wouldn't you like to sit down?"

He half turned and gave her a gracious nod. "No, thank you," he said. "I lead too sedentary a life; I prefer to stand when possible."

Claire looked at Parker. "He's at the UN," she explained, and he understood her to mean that she was sold on Gonor and wanted him to be too.

Gonor pursed his lips, as though he considered the revelation premature. "As I was saying," he said, looking back at Parker, "finding the specialist is not always easy. One knows the specialist is here, somewhere, and all one can do is sift. We — my associates and I — we required a criminal. None of us has any experience of the criminal life, at least not in this country, so we began at a disadvantage. In our search, the first prospect we turned up was Hoskins. He is a confidence man, which is the wrong specialty, but he managed to make us believe for a time that he could help us. I believe he intended merely to rob us if by chance we should prove successful."

Parker nodded. "I think that's what he was telling me," he said.

"Of course. We ultimately saw through him, naturally, and rejected him, but he seems intent on hanging around in hopes some profit will fall to him after all."

"Like a dog under the table," said the other one, who was sitting on the foot of Claire's bed, the packages all in a jumble behind him.

"Yes," Gonor said, turning toward him. "Mr Parker, this is Bara Formutesca, an assistant at the mission."

Formutesca nodded at Parker with an ironic smile. He was a younger man than Gonor, possibly in his early twenties, and beneath the red robe he seemed to have a compactly muscular body. "A pleasure," he said.

Parker nodded back at him, then looked at Gonor again. "So you went from Hoskins to Karns," he said.

"Our searching in the underworld brought us to Mr Karns's attention," Gonor said. "He sent emissaries to question us, then met with me himself, and finally suggested you. He said we could trust you but that we might have difficulty persuading you to work for us. Particularly if you had worked recently and didn't need the money."

"I don't need the money," Parker said.

Gonor pursed his lips. "Unfortunate," he said. "Still, we can only try to persuade you."

Parker turned to Claire. "Do you want to hear this?"

"I don't mind," she said. "Mr Gonor's different."

He knew she meant that Gonor didn't smell to her of violence. Violence was what frightened her, violence and the possibility of violence, which was why she didn't want to be around when Parker was planning or working on a caper, didn't want to hear about the details, didn't want to know

26

where Parker was going when he left on a job. Gonor wasn't the kind of man Parker usually worked with so she didn't think of him in connection with violence, but Parker knew she was wrong. Gonor might not be the right type for it, but now he was involved in something with the sharp metallic taste of violence all over it and he wanted Parker to get involved in it too.

But it wasn't up to him to talk her into leaving. He shrugged and said to Gonor, "All right, go ahead."

"Fine," said Gonor. But then, instead of talking, he turned away and began to pace, looking down at his feet as they touched the carpet. Pacing, looking down, he said, "Have you ever heard of Dhaba?"

"No."

Gonor nodded as he paced, as though it was the answer he'd expected. "Dhaba," he said, "is a nation. On the continent of Africa. Thirty-four months old on the first of April."

"I never heard of it," Parker said.

Formutesca, with that sardonic smile on his face again, said, "The world is full of little countries, Mr Parker. Togo, for instance. Upper Volta. Mauritania. Gabon. Mali. You don't hear of them unless they're involved in a war or a revolution. Like Yemen, or Nigeria."

Gonor said, "So far, Dhaba has had a peaceful life and has not appeared on the front pages of the world's newspapers. Unfortunately, that is soon to change."

Parker glanced at Claire, but she was watching Gonor with interest. So far it didn't mean anything to her.

Gonor said, "I have the honor to represent my country at the United Nations. Mr Formutesca here, and the other two you met, are part of the mission staff. Our nation is led by Colonel Joseph Lubudi."

"Uh huh," said Parker.

Gonor glanced at him. "You have heard of the Colonel?"

Parker said, "Hoskins mentioned a colonel. He didn't give

27

the name."

"What did he say about the Colonel?"

"That he wouldn't leave with less than a million."

Gonor looked displeased, but Formutesca laughed, saying, "Hoskins has an inflated view of our economy."

Parker said, "Every once in a while I read in the paper where the head of some little country raids the country's treasury and takes off to the Riviera. Is that what we've got here?"

"Unfortunately, yes." Gonor nodded and started his pacing again. "The Colonel has already made his raid," he said, "but he has not as yet joined his money overseas."

"The money's out of the country?"

Formutesca, his smile grim, said, "It's in New York."

"And where's the Colonel?"

"Still in Tchidanga," Gonor said, and explained, "our capital. He is not entirely trusted, and if he were to attempt abruptly to leave the country he would probably be hung from a handy lamppost."

"We have lampposts in Tchidanga," Formutesca said. "We're very proud of them."

Gonor said something to him in that other language, quick and quiet, and Formutesca suddenly looked sheepish. In English Gonor said, "Happily, we learned about our Colonel's plans in time. Dhaba will be three years old on the first of June, and ostensibly in celebration of that fact Colonel Lubudi intends to travel to New York and address the United Nations."

"They'll let him out of the country then?"

"He won't be traveling alone," Gonor said dryly. "And you can be assured his luggage will be thoroughly searched, perhaps several times."

Claire said, "Would the Colonel put up with something like that?"

Formutesca told her, "None of it will be happening out in the open."

28

"On the surface," Gonor explained, "we are all very happy and trusting toward one another."

Claire said, "Why?"

"Foreign investment," said Formutesca.

"European and American business concerns," Gonor said, "tend to pull out of African nations at the first hint of trouble. Which is only natural."

"Not only is insurrection hard on factory buildings and equipment," Formutesca added, "but revolutionary governments tend to nationalize everything they can get their hands on."

"Whatever we do," Gonor said, "must therefore be done with utmost discretion. None of us dares hint in public that we mistrust our president. None of us dares make a public move to stop his preparations for retirement at national expense. We can only try to learn his plans and keep them from happening."

Parker said, "His money's in New York. If I'm the specialist you're looking for, you want someone to steal the money back for you."

"Not exactly," Gonor said, "but very close. We didn't merely want a thief; we wouldn't ask a thief to take the risks of safeguarding our national honor for us."

Parker nodded. "Besides, he might not turn it over to you when he got it."

"Also a possibility," Gonor said. "So what we have been looking for is a planner, the sort of individual who organizes large-scale robberies."

Parker said, "You want me to plan the job?"

"Yes."

"And who does it, once I plan it?"

Gonor gestured at himself and at Formutesca. "We do. Four of us from the mission."

"Have you ever done anything like it before? Any of you?"

Gonor shook his head. "No. But we are willing to learn."

"You're amateurs who—"

There was a knock at the door. Parker saw Gonor and Formutesca tense. He turned and opened the door, and it was the other two. They came in quickly and one of them spoke to Gonor, who shook his head.

Parker said, "Gone?"

"Yes, I'm afraid so."

"He scares easy," Parker said. "That's the second time today."

"Hoskins is a cautious man," Gonor said.

"So am I," said Parker. "And so far I don't like what you're up to."

Gonor frowned. "Why not?"

"You want me to train you to do something you don't have any experience at. You've gone around talking loose talk to a lot of wrong people, telling bees all about this pot of honey you know about. So there's Hoskins buzzing around, there's this other bunch buzzing around — who are they, anyway?"

"I'm not sure," Gonor said. "They trouble me, in fact. Three white men? Unless they are from Karns . . . but I don't believe Karns would have sent me to you and then sent others to tell you not to help me."

"They had accents," Parker said. "Faint accents, maybe something like yours."

Formutesca said something, very fast. The other two looked excited and said things. Gonor shook his head, looking angry, and snapped something back at them. Then he turned away, saying, "I don't like his being involved."

"Who?" Parker said.

"General Goma," said Formutesca.

"Yes," said Gonor. He turned back to Parker. "You see," he said, "Dhaba was formed from parts of two former colonies. There were certain white factions who wanted to retain control through front men, primarily through General Goma, who was the other candidate in our first election. But Goma's connection with the whites became known and he was defeated."

Formutesca said, "There was a rumor around for a while that he was building a mercenary army, going to take over anyway, but nothing came of it."

Gonor said, "Nothing could come of it. Mercenary armies take money, and General Goma has none. His white supporters are former colonists, and of course most of their valuables stayed behind in Dhaba. Without money, General Goma is no threat."

"So he's after the diamonds too," Formutesca said.

Parker said, "Diamonds?"

"The Dhaba unit of currency," Gonor said, "is the basoko. It is not a hard currency, of course, and Colonel Lubudi naturally didn't dare ship large amounts of it out of the country. In the first place, a great quantity of basoko in the world markets would attract attention to itself. In the second place, if his defection created a sufficiently large dislocation in his wake, the basoko could quickly become valueless."

"You can't retire on yesterday's currency," said Formutesca.

"So what he did," Gonor said, "was convert basoko into real property and then reconvert that into diamonds, doing most of his conversions in South Africa."

Parker said, "Who has the diamonds?"

"The Colonel's brother-in-law, Patrick Kasempa. He is married to the Colonel's sister, making him the one person in the world the Colonel can fully trust."

"They're here in New York," Parker said, "and they have the diamonds."

"Yes."

"They have guards around the place?"

"They are well protected," Gonor said.

Parker shook his head. "What you've got here," he said, "is a very sloppy setup. The diamonds are well protected, there's other groups also after them, and you've got people like Hoskins hanging around. You'll never do it without making noise and trouble, and you probably won't come out of it with the diamonds in your possession."

"With a professional to lead us—"

"No."

Gonor looked at him. "You won't help us?"

"You can't *be* helped," Parker told him. "There's too many elements involved. The only thing for you to do is go to this Colonel and tell him you know what's up and that he won't get away with it."

Gonor shook his head. "We couldn't. If he knew we were aware of his plans, he would have no choice but to try to kill us or escape or both."

Formutesca said, "With your help, we could get the diamonds."

"No. Aside from everything else, you have a pigeon in with you."

Gonor frowned. "A what?"

"A squealer, he means," Formutesca said. "An informer. A traitor."

Parker said, "The three that were here before, the ones you said are working with this General Goma, they got here *before* you, which means they knew your plans; they didn't just follow you to me."

"Hoskins—"

"Hoskins followed *them*," Parker said. "They probably talked to him when he was working for you and found out he wasn't any threat. But since then he's kept tabs on them, which is how he got to me. Because the only name he knew for me was the one I'm registered under, but the other three knew me as Parker. That could only come from your crowd."

Gonor said, "Yes. We must have someone in our group trying to safeguard himself in case Goma should win."

"It looks that way. It also looks like they'll get to the diamonds before you do."

Gonor shook his head. "No. They'll let us do the stealing and then try to take the diamonds away from us. Because I am the only one in the group, Mr Parker, who knows where Patrick Kasempa and the diamonds are." He looked around at the others, then back at Parker. "There is no point in continuing this discussion," he said, "until we have removed the traitor. If you will excuse us now, we will call on you again at a later time."

"All right," said Parker.

Gonor said something to the others and headed for the door. The others followed him, Formutesca stopping for a second in front of Parker to say, "It isn't really as sloppy as it sounds. And we are not the total amateurs you take us for."

"That's good," Parker said.

They went out. Parker shut the door after them, turned to Claire, and said, "Pack."

6

"They're back," Claire said.

The Miami sun was straight overhead. They were having lunch in a glass-walled restaurant, the air inside cold and dry. Outside, pink and white cars with chrome slid by. Parker looked at her. "Who's back?"

She nodded at the street. Parker looked that way, and through the glass he saw three men, black, short, dressed in slacks and short-sleeved shirts, standing out there. They were in a little cluster and they seemed to be talking to one another, but the one in the middle was looking directly at Parker. It was Gonor.

Claire said, "I thought you talked to Handy."

"I did." He'd called Handy before leaving New York and told him not to give his address to the people from Dhaba any more. But here they were.

"What are you going to do?"

"I'll be back," he said, and got to his feet and went out of the restaurant. The air outside was like dirty dishcloths. Parker walked through it to the three men, Gonor in the middle. Formutesca on the left, one of the other two from the first meeting on the right.

Gonor was keeping most of the self-satisfaction from his smile. "Very hot today, Mr Parker."

"You put a tail on me."

"I'm afraid so, yes. Mr Formutesca here followed you when you left your hotel in New York."

Formutesca was letting all his self-satisfaction show. "We thought we hadn't made a good impression on you," he said, "so you might decide to go away. And that's what you did."

"We were determined," Gonor said. "to correct that impression. Keeping track of you was, you will admit, not sloppiness."

Parker nodded. "So?"

"You will also notice," Gonor said, "that we are one less than previously. We found our traitor."

"You sure he was the one?"

Gonor's smile contained a small hint of delicate savagery. "We're sure," he said.

Formutesca said, "He told us all about it before we were done."

"Where is he now?"

"He isn't," Formutesca said.

Parker looked at him. Behind the humor Formutesca looked tough. Behind the impassivity Gonor also looked tough. The third man, younger, looked strong and willing.

Gonor said, "We had hoped to bring you news of Hoskins' removal as well, but he seems to have disappeared for good this time."

"He'll be back," Formutesca said. "But probably not for a while."

Parker said, "That general and his colonist friends—"

"General Goma."

"They know you found out about their man."

"That won't make any difference," Gonor said. "They won't move against us until they believe we have the diamonds."

Parker turned and looked at the restaurant. Claire was sitting in there on the cool side of the glass, watching. She nodded when their eyes met. He turned back to Gonor and said, "Why follow me? I gave you a no up in New York when I left."

"Because you had the wrong impression of us," Gonor said. "If you say no to us after we have corrected that impression, of course we will no longer bother you."

"We want to give you the proposition first," Formutesca said. "We never got to that in New York."

"You want me to plan your heisting the diamonds."

Gonor frowned. "Heisting?"

Formutesca grinned at him. "Stealing," he explained, then said to Parker, "I went to M.I.T. Mr Gonor learned his English in school."

Gonor was irritated. "M.I.T. is a school," he snapped. Then to Parker he said, "The proposition is this. We will pay you twenty-five thousand dollars, plus expenses, to plan the robbery and train us to perform it, the money payable on the eve of the robbery before we do it and yours whether the robbery succeeds or not."

"You don't want me along."

"Not unless it's absolutely necessary," Gonor said. "Which would be, of course, your decision. If you feel your physical presence during the robbery will be necessary, we will pay you an additional twenty-five thousand dollars. At the same time as the first."

"You'll give me the layout?"

"Naturally."

"What if I look at it and decide it can't be done?"

"We'll pay your expenses up to that point," Gonor said, "and thank you for your opinion."

Parker watched the traffic. "Where are you staying?"

Gonor grimaced. "At a place called the Sunrise Motel."

"For colored," Formutesca said, amused.

"If I call at eight o'clock tonight," Parker said, "it means yes. If I don't, it means no."

"Fair enough," Gonor said. "We'll hope to hear from you."

Parker nodded and turned away and went back into the restaurant. The air inside was too cold for comfort now, chilling the sweat on his face and back. He sat down at the table and Claire smiled knowingly at him, saying, "You're going to do it."

36

"Maybe," Parker said.

"They got your interest," she said. "You'll do it."

"Maybe," Parker said.

7

Claire said, "What time is it?"

They were in their room. Parker looked at his watch and said, "Five to eight."

"Are you going to call?"

"You want me to do it," he said.

She nodded. "Yes, I do."

"We don't need the money."

"I know. But we will in six months, and what you're offered in six months probably won't be as good."

He shook his head and walked around the room trying to think. "Good?" he said. "What do you mean, good? We don't know whether it's good or bad yet, we don't know where the diamonds are, what the security is—"

"You know what I mean," she said.

"You think it's a good cause," he said.

"Yes."

"I don't do things for good causes."

"I know," she said. "So you do it because of the money, and I'll be glad you're doing it because it's a good cause."

"I couldn't say yes for sure at this point," Parker said. "All I could say is I'd look at it."

"I know. You have to be interested, too; it's never just the money."

He knew she was wrong about that, that at times he'd gone into jobs for the money and nothing else, but it was true that it helped to have work he could take an interest in. And it would be interesting to plan a job for amateurs, to take the specifics of the situation and make them work in his favor.

The part of him that took pleasure in professionalism, in craft, was already half involved in this project, anxious to find out the rest of the details.

But there were things against it too. They *were* amateurs, no matter how tough or how willing. And they *had* spread the news around a little too much, so that the job was complicated with Hoskins and General Goma and the ex-colonists and who knew how many others.

There was a silence as he paced, thinking about it, until Claire said, "And I'd like to come along."

He stopped and frowned at her. "What do you mean, come along?"

"It's in New York, isn't it? That's where you'll have to be while they're getting ready."

"You don't want to be part of it."

"No. But we could live together during it. It wouldn't be like the times when you're doing it yourself."

"I might have to," he said.

Sharply she said, "Why? That isn't what they want to hire you for."

"It might be necessary, it might not."

"What, lead your troops into battle? All they want is a teacher and a planner."

"I'm telling you it's a possibility."

She bit her lip, hesitated, then made a half-angry shrug of dismissal. "All right. Even so."

"I wouldn't want you part of it," he said. "Not present during the meetings, not anything."

"Neither would I," she said. "But we could be together in between times." She smiled, saying, "Besides, my shopping trip was interrupted. It'll give me something to do."

Parker walked over to the window. The hotel's shadow stretched across the sea, and the sky at the far horizon was already black with night. Behind him, Claire said, "It's eight o'clock."

"I know."

"You want me to look up their number?"

What could he lose? He'd look at their situation. "Sunrise Motel," he said.

Two

1

"Come in," said Gonor. "This way."

Parker followed him through the apartment. The furnishings were new, discreet, anonymous and expensive, with all the earmarks of things purchased by a hired decorator at stores with the notice in their windows: TO THE TRADE ONLY. As they went through, on one wall Parker saw a rough-textured painting of Negro dancers in front of some kind of yellowish hut, and on another wall there was a carved ebony mask, but aside from these there was no indication that the occupants of this apartment were Africans or had ever heard of Africa, so that finally the painting and the mask blended in with the rest, looking like just two more items that had caught the decorator's eye.

The sitting-room they wound up in was done in quiet shades of green and gray and had windows overlooking Fifth Avenue and Central Park. Formutesca and the third man from Miami were sitting on the green sofa to the right. An older man, very black and with thick white hair, was standing at the window looking thoughtfully at the park as though seeing something else. He and Gonor were in Western dress, Formutesca and the other man in the red robes of their first meeting.

Gonor said, speaking to the older man, "This is Parker."

The older man turned his head and studied Parker tiredly and suspiciously. His manner was that of a sage that people don't come to any more.

Parker said to Gonor, "How many more?"

Gonor looked at him in surprise. "How many more what?"

"People. First there were four of you, and one was no

43

good. Plus Hoskins, General Goma, Goma's ex-colonist friends, Karns from the syndicate, and now this one. How many more people are on the inside of this thing?"

Gonor was shocked. "Major Indindu is in charge!"

"In charge of what?"

The older man showed a thin smile. "Your surprise is natural, Mr Parker," he said. He had a heavily British accent. "As is your mistrust. As, I hope you will agree, is my mistrust."

"The Major will be our next president," Gonor said.

Parker looked at him. "You mean, after the Colonel's out?"

Major Indindu said, "If we succeed in restoring the stolen assets, we will allow Colonel Lubudi to announce his retirement during his stay in New York. A new election will be held in Dhaba, and after I am elected, the Colonel will be free either to return or to stay in New York."

Parker said, "What if you're not elected?"

"I will be."

Gonor said fervently, "Major Indindu is our only hope!"

"All right. What about the situation? The diamonds, and how they're protected."

"That's too fast, Mr Parker," said the Major.

Parker looked at Gonor. "Up to now," he said, "I've dealt with you. If this thing takes place, you'll be doing the robbery. Is that right?"

Gonor nodded.

"Who else?"

"Mr Formutesca and Mr Manado."

"Manado?"

Gonor gestured to the man sitting beside Formutesca. "I'm sorry, I thought I had introduced you on our first meeting."

"What about the Major?" Parker said.

Gonor was surprised again. "With us on the robbery? Naturally not!"

44

"Then he doesn't belong here."

"Surely you can trust—"

"It isn't trust or not trust. We're not here for a party, we're here to do a thing. Anybody who isn't involved in doing that thing shouldn't be here."

"The Major had to approve you before—"

"No," Parker said. "You're the man who's going out on the limb; you're the one who'll make it or lose on the basis of how good I am. What the Major has to do is take your word about me and keep out of our way."

The Major said something in his native tongue. Gonor, looking unhappy, said something back to him. The Major said something else.

There was a whole conversation starting there. Parker turned away and went over to Formutesca and Manado. Manado was looking slightly shocked and slightly scared, but Formutesca was looking amused.

Parker said to Manado, "How old are you?"

He'd been listening to the Major and Gonor, and now he blinked, focused on Parker, and said, "Sir? I beg your pardon?"

"How old are you?"

"Twenty-three, sir."

Parker turned to Formutesca. "You?"

Formutesca was smiling happily. "Thirty-one," he said.

"You both went to college?"

"Yes, sir," said Manado, and Formutesca nodded.

"Do any sports?"

"Track team, sir," said Manado.

"Baseball," said Formutesca. "Third base. And some gymnastics."

"You know how to handle guns?"

"Yes, sir," said Manado, and Formutesca said:

"Naturally."

"Why naturally?"

"Not all of Dhaba is in the twentieth century,"

45

Formutesca said.

The conversation between Gonor and the Major seemed to have ended, but Parker kept his attention on these two in front of him. He said, "That means you know rifles. Anything else?"

"I have fired handguns," said Manado. "And the Sten and Uzi."

"Me too," said Formutesca.

"What languages do you speak?"

"Just Abu and English," said Manado.

"Abu? That's your native tongue?"

"Yes, sir."

Formutesca said, "I speak some French, some German. More French."

A door closed. Parker said, "You both drive? You have licenses to drive in this country?" They both nodded. "Either of you color-blind? Epileptic? Get fainting spells? You got any phobias, fear of heights or anything like that?" They both kept shaking their heads.

Behind Parker, Gonor said, "Mr Parker."

Parker turned around. Gonor was alone. "The Major has approved you," he said, and it was possible there was something humorous in his tone.

"Good," said Parker.

"We'll go for a drive now," Gonor said.

"Why?"

"I'll show you where the diamonds are."

2

The car was a black Mercedes-Benz. Manado was at the wheel and Formutesca beside him, with Gonor and Parker in back. "Go down Park Avenue," Gonor had said, so Manado had driven down Fifth Avenue to the first eastbound street, over two blocks to Park, and they were now headed south, the Pan Am Building hulking in the roadway ahead of them.

"This will be interesting to our young friends as well," Gonor said, nodding at the two in front. "They still don't know where the Kasempas are keeping themselves and the diamonds."

Gonor should have kept his security as tight as that on the whole deal, but Parker didn't say so. He just nodded and looked out the window at the cabs.

After a minute Gonor said, "You don't think much of Major Indindu."

"I don't think anything of him. I don't think about him at all."

Gonor frowned, studying Parker. "Is that true? Is that why you're successful? You ignore whatever is not directly necessary?"

"You can't think about more than one thing at a time," Parker said.

"Granted," said Gonor.

"Do I continue, sir?" Manado asked. The Pan Am Building was looming up directly ahead, like a life-sized model no longer needed and left out in the street for the Sanitation Department to take away.

"Straight on," Gonor said. "But don't take the tunnel."

Manado steered the car around the racetrack ramp girdling

Grand Central Terminal, of which the Pan Am Building is the hat. He drove well but a trifle too cautiously, letting himself be outbluffed occasionally by hustling cabbies.

They came down the ramp to Fortieth Street, avoided the tunnel underpass, and Gonor said, "Turn left at Thirty-eighth Street."

Formutesca turned around, saying, "The museum?"

Gonor nodded to him.

"Nobody lives there," Formutesca said.

"There is the top-floor apartment."

"But . . . nobody *ever* lived there!"

"Not till now," Gonor said. Turning to Parker he said, "Seven Central African nations, when they were all colonies of the same European power, combined to create and support a Museum of African Arts and Artifacts in New York City. Actually it was the mother country that was the inspiration and most of the fnancial support for the museum. As each of the colonies became independent it ceased to be a supporting member of the museum. Until us. We were the last of the colonies to gain independence. Rather than take over the museum itself, which would have been at the least anomalous, our former mother country has given the museum to us and has presented us with a fund from which the proceeds will furnish the operating expenses."

Manada had been stopped by a red light at Thirty-ninth Street, but now it turned green and he drove forward a block and made his left. Gonor looked out the windshield and said, "Park across the street."

"Don't stop," Parker said. "Just go past it slow."

Gonor looked at him in surprise. "Wouldn't you care to study it for a period of time?"

"Yes, but I don't want the people in it to be studying me."

"Oh. I'm sorry; that hadn't occurred to me."

"That's why you hired me," Parer said. "Where is it?"

"Just ahead, on the left," Gonor said.

Parker looked out the window and saw it as they drove by.

A narrow building of gray stone, it was set back from the sidewalk and separated from its neighbors by narrow alleys on both sides. A black wrought-iron fence, waist high, ran across the front of the property, with carefully tended grass and trees behind it, flanking the walk up to the building itself, which was four stories high. The windows on the first two floors were barred. The front door was massive dark wood, and on the stone wall beside it was a square plaque, unreadable from here. The place looked well cared for but empty. The rest of the buildings on the block were either quiet residential hotels or old town houses converted to discreet offices.

"All right," Parker said. "Turn right on Lexington."

"Why not go back?" Gonor said.

"In traffic like this," Parker told him, "there's no way to be sure you're not being followed. You've been followed in the past, sometimes by Hoskins, sometimes by General Goma's people. So maybe you're being followed now, and if you are we don't want them to know we're interested in that museum."

"Good," said Gonor.

The light at the corner was green. Manado made the turn. Parker told him, "When you get to Twenty-third Street make the left. Go over to Third Avenue and then south. When you get to Twelfth Street circle the block to the east and keep an eye on the rearview mirror, see if anybody follows you around."

"Yes, sir," said Manado.

Parker said to Gonor, "Tell me about this building."

"It's a museum," Gonor said. "Three floors of African artifacts, from shields and spears to wooden dolls. And a fully-equipped apartment on the top floor."

"That nobody's ever lived in?"

"It was planned to have a full-time curator," Gonor said, "but there was never any need for it. And lately, since Dhaba became independent, the museum has been virtually closed.

49

We have a notice on the front door saying the museum is open by appointment only and giving my office phone number to call. There are still occasionally scholars of one sort or another interested in having a look. When one of them calls, either I or one of my staff will come by, unlock the place, and show the visitor around."

"That's the only time anybody goes in there?"

"We have a commercial cleaning service, which goes through the display rooms once a week. Also a grounds-keeping service, but they don't actually enter the building."

Formutesca twisted around again to say to Parker, "The museum isn't exactly the liveliest place in town."

"It was a bad idea to begin with," Gonor said, "and is now outdated as well."

"But Patrick Kasempa is living there."

"Yes. I discovered them almost by accident over a month ago. An anthropologist from the University of Pennsylvania had asked to see some items in our musical instrument department. He spent most of the afternoon. It was getting dark when we left, and that evening I realized I'd left a pipe behind. I went back for it, and there were lights in the top-floor windows. We had been looking for the Kasempas for two or three weeks before that, ever since our friends at home had let us know about the plot, so I waited around to see if anyone appeared. Within half an hour Lucille Kasempa came walking down the street, apparently returning from shopping."

"Did she see you?"

"No."

"It's just the two of them in there?"

"Not at all," Gonor said. "Patrick Kasempa is one of four brothers, all of whom disappeared at the same time. My guess is the other three are in there with him. On guard duty, you might say."

Parker nodded. "How many ways into the building?" he asked.

50

"Well, the front door," Gonor said. "And a back door, of course; the Fire Department insisted. But it is metal and very securely fastened on the inside. There was a fear of burglaries, the building being empty so much of the time."

"What's in back?"

"Not much of anything. At one time it was arranged as a small garden back there with some outdoor sculpture. But it wasn't authentic; the sculpture was metal casts from wood originals, the flora was wrong and so on, so it was given up."

"How do you get out there? Just through the house?"

"Yes."

Formutesca said, "There's a fence at the back, a wooden fence about eight feet high. If you wanted to, you could come through a buiding on Thirty-ninth Street and over that fence."

Manado said, "Sir?"

Gonor said, "What?"

Manado was looking at Parker in the rearview mirror. "We are being followed," he said, "by a white Chevrolet Corvair containing two men. I can't make them out clearly."

"Go around a few blocks," Parker said. "Lose them."

"Yes, sir."

To Gonor Parker said, "What about the side alleys? Can you get to the back through them?"

"There are iron gates at the rear corners of the building," Gonor said. "They are usually kept locked."

"Can you get me blueprints of the building?"

"Naturally."

"And floor plans showing where the displays are."

"We have those, yes."

"Good." Parker frowned out the window a minute, then turned back to Gonor and said, "You know you're going to have to kill."

"Not necessarily," Gonor said.

"Yes," Parker said. "There are four brothers up there.

51

You won't get in without killing at least one, and that means you have to kill all four. And the wife."

Smiling bleakly from the front seat, Formutesca said, "We already knew that, Mr Parker. We weren't sure you knew it. Or what your attitude would be."

"It just means you've got to look out for the local law too," Parker said.

"Anything that occurs," Gonor said, "will occur in our building. We are unlikely to make a complaint."

"Then noise is a problem too," said Parker.

Formutesca, smiling, said, "We can be quiet."

Manado said, "The white Corvair is no longer following us." He sounded proud of himself.

"Good," Parker said. "Take me back to my hotel."

3

Lying on his back on the floor, Parker fixed the holster to the underside of the bed. A .22-caliber High Standard Sentinel fit in there snugly, but would slide out without trouble. With the pistol in place, Parker got to his feet and saw Claire frowning at him. She said, "You've never done that before." "I do it when I'm working." He hadn't told her about the Corvair.

"We're at a different hotel," she said. "We're using a different name."

"I like to be careful," Parker said. His other gun, a Browning .380 automatic, was on the bed. He picked it up and put it on the shelf in the closet, under the extra blanket. The Terrier he'd bought the last time he was in New York he'd gotten rid of as soon as he'd left the city. It was cheaper and safer in the long run to buy your guns as you needed them and get rid of them as soon as they were no longer necessary.

Watching him, Claire said, "Are they back again?"

Parker carried a chair over to the hall door and leaned it so it would fall over if the door was opened. "Who?" he said.

"Those three men. The ones we saw first."

"I haven't seen them," he said. He went into the bathroom, came out with a glass, put it on the windowsill, and leaned against the window.

Claire had lit a cigarette. She was moving nervously around the room, studying Parker and shaking her head. "There's something," she said. "You don't do all this every time. You think they might come after us."

Parker turned and looked at her. "Sure they might," he said. "There's a country they used to run and now they don't.

53

They want to run it again, and to run it they need to put their front man Goma in power, and to do that they need money, and that means the diamonds, and that means they don't want me involved. So they might come around."

She bit her lip. "You want me to leave," she said.

"Yes. I was going to tell you in the morning."

"You want me to go back to Miami?"

"No. In the morning you take a cab out to Kennedy Airport. Then you take another cab back, and you take a room at a different hotel under some other name. We'll work out what hotel, what name."

"Why?" she said.

"Your shopping trip. You can go on—"

"No," she said. "You don't give a damn about my shopping trip."

He hesitated, then said, "All right. I don't want them to lean on me through you."

"All you had to do was say so," she said. "I guessed it a long time ago."

He shrugged. "What hotel do you want to stay at?"

"The thing is," she said, smiling at him now, "you worry about me, and you don't like it that you worry about me. You don't want me to see it."

Parker shrugged again, irritated. "Whatever you say."

"So why don't I shop in Boston?" she said. "Do you know the Herridge House there?"

"No."

"It's a nice hotel, very small. I'll be Miss Carol Bowen."

"Mrs," he said.

"Oh, of course. Because you'll be coming along later." She stepped forward and put her hand on his arm. "Not much later, will you?"

"I don't know how long it will take," he said. "A week, maybe a month."

"Then we should start saying goodbye now," she said.

4

It was like an art gallery: blueprints, floor plans, and photos all along the walls. Parker moved slowly from one to the next, an interested patron of the arts.

Gonor had set up this one room of his apartment as a kind of headquarters or war room. He'd stripped it to a table and four chairs under the central light fixture, he'd put the blueprints and other material along the walls, and on the table he'd put pads and pencils. He moved with Parker now, pointing out specific items of interest on the different floor plans.

"The fire escape," he said at one point, tapping the paper. "On the rear of the building."

"Can we use it?" Manado and Formutesca were sitting at the table, watching and waiting.

Gonor shook his head. "No. The windows opening on to it are protected by metal gates on the inside."

Parker nodded and kept looking. A minute later he tapped the blueprint he was looking at and said, "Elevator?"

"Yes."

"Mm." Parker moved on. "Basement," he said. "Any exterior way in?"

"No. There was at one time a coal chute on the left side of the building near the front, but that was removed and the window covered when the building was converted to the museum."

"Window covered how?"

"With masonry."

"All right."

There were photos of the building, front and back. The

front showed him nothing he didn't already know, and the back looked like a prison with its barred windows and black metal door. There were some photos of the interior, various display rooms.

"Those are stock photos," Gonor said. "We've had them on file for some time; they're to be used in publicity and news releases."

"They're out of date?"

Gonor shook his head. "Nothing changes inside the museum," he said. "It still looks like that today."

Parker studied the pictures, then nodded and turned away and sat down at the table. Gonor sat at his left, with Formutesca opposite and Manado on the right.

Parker said, "About the elevator. What's at the top of the shaft?"

Gonor had no idea what he was talking about. "The roof," he said, surprised.

"There's got to be the motor housing," Parker told him. "Or is that in the basement?"

"Oh, I see, yes. Yes, it's in the basement. But there is some machinery at the top." He twisted around and pointed to the picture of the rear of the building. "You see that black shape on top of the building there?"

"How do you get into it?"

Gonor frowned, studying the picture from his seat. "I don't remember. But I'm sure there's some way."

"I think the top is hinged," Formutesca said. "It's only about three feet by four."

"Kept locked?"

Gonor said, "Oh, certainly."

"But you have a key."

Gonor frowned. "I suppose so. I'm sure we must."

"What's the problem?"

"In my desk drawer at the mission," Gonor said. "I have a yellow envelope marked *Museum Keys*, with a dozen or more keys inside. Which key is which I have no idea."

56

"We'll have to find out," Parker said.

Formutesca said, "You can't get to the roof without going through the fourth floor. They'll never let us do it."

"That's right," Gonor said. "We could go there, and so long as we stayed in the museum area the Kasempas would leave us alone. In fact, they'd be silent; they'd hide the fact of their existence. But if we went to the fourth floor they wouldn't be able to hide any more. And they know I am one of those opposed to Colonel Lubudi."

Parker said, "How far would they go?"

"They would kill us," Gonor said. "Kill us and bury the bodies in the basement. So the Negro head of the mission of an obscure and tiny African state disappears in New York. We might be in the local papers for two or three days, some of the more rabid Communist nations might get a little propaganda value out of American lawlessness, but that would be all."

"All right," Parker said. "But we have to know about the elevator shaft first."

"But why?"

"We can't get in at the front," Parker told him. "And we can't get in at the back or the sides. With the coal-chute window sealed off, we can't get in at the bottom. That leaves the top."

Formutesca laughed, a sudden bark of delight. "That's the kind of thinking we want!" he said.

Gonor smiled at Formutesca, then said to Parker, "Several years ago I read a detective story, English or American, I'm not sure which. In it, the detective advocated eliminating all impossibilities. Whatever was left, he said, however improbable, was the truth. Now I find the other side of the law has a similar dictum. The only problem is, how do we get *to* the top?"

"From next door," Parker said. He got to his feet and went over to the picture showing the front of the house. "You've got about four feet here," he said, pointing to the alley to the

57

left of the house. "And the same on the other side. The buildings on both sides are taller than this one. We go out a window from one of those buildings and over to the roof."

Gonor said, "How?"

"It depends on the position of the window in relation to the roof. If we can, we'll just put a one-by-twelve across from the sill to the roof. If the angle's too steep, we'll have to do it with ropes and grappling irons."

Formutesca said, "What about the people over there? We'd rather not cause trouble with innocent bystanders."

"We'll be going at night," Parker said. "We'll have to find a place that's empty at night. That's no problem."

Formutesca grinned. "If you say so," he said.

Parker went back to the table and sat down. "The next thing is armaments," he said. "Can we get whatever we need?"

"Within reason," Gonor said. "I couldn't get us a tank or a helicopter, for instance. But I can get guns, rifles, machine guns."

"Gas?"

"What kind of gas?"

"Knockout. Stuff that works fast and disperses fast."

Gonor smiled bitterly. "I'm not sure that's among the items the big boys will let us play with," he said. When Parker frowned at him, he explained, "All our armaments come from the major nations, of course. And Israel, which in some ways is also a major nation. But there are agreements among the arms-producing nations about which armaments will be sold in which part of the world. We, for instance, may purchase jet fighters from anyone, and so we have an air force of seven MIG-fifteens and five F-ninety-fours, all purchased used, but no one will sell us a jet bomber."

Parker said, "Whatever we want you're going to have to have shipped from Dhaba?"

"Not at all," Gonor said. "Mr Formutesca is our military attaché. He will make the purchases in this country for

58

shipment to our warehouse space in Newark, and after that whatever items we need just won't go on to Dhaba." Gonor shrugged. "Simplicity," he said.

Parker said to Formutesca, "Can you get the gas?"

"I'll have to check," Formutesca said. "I doubt they'll let us have that kind of lethal gas."

"It doesn't have to be lethal. All it has to do is knock a man out in one or two breaths."

"Non-lethal? I'm sure we can get that."

"Good. We'll also need some sort of explosive. One that won't cause much damage but makes a big bang."

Formutesca nodded. "I know something good for that."

To Gonor Parker said, "Can you get more pictures of the outside of the house without being seen?"

"I think so," Gonor said.

"I want angle shots," Parker said. "So I can see the sides of the flanking buildings."

"All right."

"If you can't get them without tipping yourself to the people inside, let it go."

"I'll be careful," Gonor said.

"Good. Formutesca, have you got old clothes? Very sloppy old clothes."

"I have the things I play touch football in."

"They have to look like work clothes. Like a janitor."

"Oh! Yes, of course. I have a pair of trousers so smeared with paint they'd pass for a Pollock."

"Good." To Gonor he said, "We're going to need a truck, a small delivery van. The smaller the better."

"I'm afraid we don't own a truck," Gonor said.

"Then buy one. Old. Used. As old as you can get."

Gonor nodded. "We can do that."

"When you've got it," Parker said, "give me a call. And Formutesca, you be ready with the old clothes."

Smiling, pleased, Formutesca nodded. "I will," he said.

Parker got to his feet. "That's all for now," he said. "If

you've got a cleaning lady, take that stuff off the walls."

"I'm keeping this room locked," Gonor said.

"All right."

Gonor walked him to the door. "I believe you're a good teacher," he said. "And I believe you will find us quick students."

"That's good," Parker said.

5

Hoskins got to his feet when Parker came into the room. The gun in his right hand was small but efficient-looking. Parker took his key out of the lock and shut the door. He dropped the key on the dresser and shrugged out of his coat. Hoskins watched him, a faintly pleasant expression on his face, attempting to be the club man meeting an old friend at the club. The gun spoiled the effect, and so did the wariness he couldn't keep from showing in his eyes.

Parker tossed his coat on the bed, and Hoskins flinched, just a little. If he was that nervous, he might fire the gun by accident. To calm him down a little, Parker talked softly to him, saying, "Somebody let you in?"

Hoskins had control of himself again. "No, no, dear boy," he said. "One picks up keys here and there, you know. They fit a variety of locks."

The "dear boy" was new. Parker, looking closely at him, now saw that Hoskins was drunk. Quietly drunk, in a steady and dignified way. Full of what he himself undoubtedly would call Dutch courage.

Parker turned toward the bathroom. "You want a drink?"

"I think not. You're playing with Gonor and that crowd, aren't you?"

Parker stopped and looked at him. "Playing?"

"On their team."

Parker shrugged.

"The only question is," Hoskins said, "did you send those two cannibals down to the bar after me that day or didn't you?"

Parker said, "That isn't the question."

"It isn't? Really, dear boy. What *is* the question, then?"

Parker said, "How to keep you from coming back."

Hoskins opened his mouth to laugh. "But you can't," he said. "I have the smell of gold in my nostrils now."

"You want a piece."

"Of course. But not for nothing; I'm not like that. I can contribute, you know."

"Contribute what?"

"Myself. My expertise, for what it's worth. Because whatever you may think of Gonor and his lieutenants, dear boy, you should never underestimate them. You won't get the booty away from them all by yourself, you know."

Parker said, "What if I'm not going to take it away from them at all?"

Hoskins made a mocking face, lifting one eyebrow. "What, settle for twenty-five thousand? You don't look that sort of man to me, Mr Walker."

"I'll tell you another sort of man I'm not," Parker said. "I don't do business with a man holding a gun on me."

Hoskins looked at the gun in his hand as though mildly surprised to see it still there. Shrugging, he smiled amiably and said, "I didn't know what your attitude would be, of course. I had to be ready to protect myself in case you were going to be difficult."

"I won't be difficult," Parker said, "if you can be reasonable. And useful. We should be able to work something out."

There was relief evident in Hoskins' smile now. "I thought you were a sensible man," he said. "I thought we could get together."

Parker pointed at the gun. "Not with that in your hand," he said. "Put it away."

"Of course," said Hoskins. "Sorry, old man." He tucked the gun away in his hip pocket.

Parker walked over toward him, hand extended for a shake, saying, "Now we can start a partnership."

Hoskins was delighted. "Bound to be a profitable one," he said, and put his hand out for Parker's. Parker hit him high on the right cheek and he fell backward over the bed and landed on his side on the floor. Parker walked around the bed and kicked Hoskins once. Hoskins fell back and didn't move.

Parker went to one knee and emptied Hoskins' pockets, beginning with the gun, a Beretta .22 automatic, lethal at arm's length but not much good beyond that. In the other hip pocket was a wallet. Hoskins had two Diner's Club cards, one in the name of Fields, one in the name of Goldstein. He also had fifty-three dollars in cash, a California driver's license giving his name as Wilfred R. Hoskins, a wallet calendar from a New York City bank giving formulas for finding Manhattan addresses on the back, and a baggage claim check from Penn Station.

Parker tossed the wallet on the bed, rolled Hoskins over, and went through the rest of his pockets. A pack of Salem cigarettes, a Zippo lighter engraved with the word *Burma*, a key to room 627 at the Edward Hotel, Broadway and Seventy-second Street, the return of a round-trip United Air Lines ticket from Los Angeles, date open, a switchblade knife, a small packet of tissues, a key pouch containing half a dozen keys, including one to a General Motors car, and a small notebook with its own short ballpoint pen inside. In the notebook there was a crossed-out notation of the name and address Parker had had the last time he was up in New York — Matthew Walker, Room 723, Normanton Hotel — and beneath it the name and address this time — Thomas Lynch, Room 516, Winchester Hotel. On another page there were four names in descending order, followed by an address:

Goma
Jock Daask
Avon Marten
Robert Quilp
193 Riverside Drive, Apt. 7-J

Parker went back to Hoskins' wallet, checked the back of the bank calendar, and found 193 Riverside Drive would be around West Ninety-first Street. Too far north to be a first-rate address.

Hoskins made a sound in his throat and moved his head a little. Parker put everything back in his pockets except the notebook and the Beretta, which he put away in a dresser drawer.

Hoskins was stirring now. Parker went over and grabbed him under the arms and dragged him over to the window. He opened the window, and March air rushed in, cold and wet. He lifted Hoskins and turned him so his chest was on the windowsill and his head hung out the window. West Forty-fourth Street was five stories down.

"Wake up," Parker said, and reached over Hoskins' shoulder to slap his face.

The slap and the cold air finished the job of bringing Hoskins around. Parker had his other hand on Hoskins' back holding him in place, and he felt him stiffen when his eyes opened and he saw nothing but air beneath him for fifty feet.

Hoskins struggled, trying to get back in, but Parker held him there like a moth pinned to a display board. Hoskins was calling things out there, amazed things and terrified things.

Parker waited till Hoskins settled down a little, then he dragged him back in. Hoskins' face was bright red, as though paint had been poured on it. "For God's sake," he said. "For God's sake." He was sober.

Parker said, "The next time you come around, I don't bring you back in."

"For God's sake, man." Hoskins was touching himself all over — tie, cheek, belt, hair, mouth — as though to reassure himself he was still there. "You didn't have to—"

"You wouldn't listen to me. Will you listen to me now?"

"Of course, man. Good God, you don't have to—"

"Then listen." Parker stood in front of him and spoke slowly and carefully, looking into Hoskins' frightened eyes.

64

"I am working with Gonor," he said. "I am taking the cut he offered me. I am not taking anything else and I am not helping you take anything else. Do you understand that?"

Hoskins had begun to blink rapidly, the prelude to shaky defiance, an attempt to get back his self-esteem. "I understand," he said. Then, very high and fast, "Oh, I understand, don't you worry. You want the whole thing for yourself, that's plain enough. Well, you can have it, for all the good it'll do you. You're as crazy as those black madmen and you deserve each other and I hope before you're done you'll *all* kill each other off, because they won't be as easy to fool as you think, they'll be on to—"

Parker slaped him, open-handed, just hard enough to stop the flow of words. "You didn't listen," he said.

Hoskins put his hand to his cheek. "I said I was out," he said as though some great injustice had just been done him.

Parker looked at him and considered. Keep pushing and convince him of the truth? There was no point in it, not if he'd been sufficiently convinced to keep himself away from the action. In fact, it might be better if he thought Parker greedy enough to try for the whole pie himself. Hoskins would tend to stay a long way away from the kind of fight a Parker and a Gonor could have together.

Parker nodded and stepped back. "Good," he said. "You're out. Use that ticket to L.A."

Hoskins felt for it in his jacket pocket in quick panic, and showed relief when it was still there. Then he felt the rest of his pockets and became aggrieved. "My gun!" he cried. "My notebook!"

"You don't need a gun," Parker told him. "Not on the plane."

"My notebook."

"You don't need to take notes."

"Listen," Hoskins said, getting loud, "you can't do—"

Parker turned away from him and went over and opened the hall door. "Goodbye," he said.

65

"You can't—" Hoskins said. "You can't just—"

"I don't want to have to touch you," Parker said.

Hoskins looked like a man who wanted very much to start punching something. But all he did was stand there rocking slightly on the balls of his feet and glaring at Parker in helpless rage.

Parker started toward him from the door.

"I'm going," Hoskins said, trying not to sound too hasty. "Don't worry, I'm going. Back to L.A. I wouldn't be involved in this—"

"That's good."

"But you'll regret it, mark my words. You'll wish you had a man you could trust at your side."

Parker didn't say anything to that. Hoskins looked anxiously around trying to find something else to say, but there wasn't any more. He shook his head, tried to put on the scowling expression of a patrician leaving by his own choice and walked past Parker and out of the room.

Parker shut the door after him.

6

It was a half-ton Ford panel truck, seven years old, dark blue. Some previous owner's firm name and address and phone number had been painted off the doors and body sides with broad sweeps of paler blue, itself old enough now to be chipped in places. Parker was at the wheel, Formutesca beside him, and he was finding the transmission almost unworkable. But the truck wouldn't be needed long, and it would never be asked to travel very far or very fast, so it would do.

Formutesca was wearing his paint-smeared trousers, an old flannel shirt, an old brown leather jacket with ragged elbows and cuffs, and old brown shoes. Parker was in a suit and topcoat, but had his tie loose and his shirt collar open.

They turned into Thirty-eighth Street from Park Avenue and found a parking space just up the block from the museum. Parker cut the ignition, pocketed the key, and said to Formutesca, "You ready?"

"I think I have stage fright," Formuesca said with a slightly shaky smile. "But I'll be all right."

"Good," Parker said. He picked up the clipboard from the seat between them and got out of the truck. He waited on the sidewalk while Formutesca went around to the rear of the truck and got the toolbox and the seven-foot stepladder.

"Heavy," Formutesca said, grinning shakily.

"All you have to do," Parker told him, "is look sullen and stupid."

"At this hour," Formutesca said, "that should be easy." It was a little after two in the morning.

Parker led the way down the sidewalk to the building just

this side of the museum. The pictures Gonor had taken showed this one to be the better bet of the two. The other was a residential hotel, but this one was primarily an office building, with very few twenty-four-hour tenants. Also, the windows in this building's fifth floor seemed to be at just about the right height, and two of them side by side were of frosted glass, surely meaning rest rooms.

There was a green canopy out front. Parker went under it, pushed open the door, held it for Formutesca, then went over and pushed the bell button beside the word *Superintendent*. When nothing happened after half a minute he rang again, and this time there came a response, a garbled voice sputtering out of the speaker above the buttons. The words couldn't be made out, but the meaning was clear; he wanted to know who it was.

Parker leaned close to the speaker. "Water supply," he said. He sounded bored and irritated.

"*Wha?*"

"Water supply," Parker said, louder.

"*Whadaya want?*"

"We gotta get in."

There was a pause, and then a grudging, "*Hold on.*"

They waited nearly five minutes, and then a short and heavyset man appeared at the end of the corridor inside. He was wearing a maroon robe, brown pants and slippers, and he walked in a heavy-footed waddle. He came slowly down to the glass doors, looked through them at Parker and Formutesca, then opened one door and said, "You people know what time it is?"

"We don't like it any better than you do," Parker said. "If they'd done it right the first time, we wouldn't have to be here on any emergency call."

"What emergency call? I didn't call nobody."

"Not you," Parker said. He walked through the doorway, Formutesca behind him. "The City," Parker said. "It's that fifth-floor men's room again."

"What do you mean, again?" The superintendent was still half asleep; he was irritated, and he was bewildered. But he wasn't suspicious.

"It was supposed to be fixed three months ago," Parker said. He consulted his clipboard. "Some smart inspector said it was all taken care of."

"What inspector?"

Parker frowned suspiciously at him. "Didn't you get that men's room fixed?" he asked. "Three months ago?"

The superintendent shook his head, befuddled. "There's nothing wrong with any men's room in here," he said. "There hasn't been."

"Oh, yeah?" Parker jabbed a thumb at the street. "You almost had a water main blow up out there, that's how much there's nothing wrong."

The superintendent looked toward the street, then back at Parker. "I don't know a thing about it," he said.

"Yeah," said Parker, showing disgust. "You know what that means, don't you? Somebody layin' down on the job. Nobody came around here three months ago, that's what happened."

"Sure it is," the superintendent said, happy to have something he could be knowledgeable about. "Nobody came around at all."

"That's what I mean," Parker said. He shook his head. "All right," he said, "let's get the damn thing done right this time. Is it locked up there?"

"No. I'll take you up."

"Good."

Parker felt Formutesca trying to catch his eye, but the worst thing you could do in a situation like this was step out of character. Parker faced front and followed the superintendent down the hall to the elevator, Formutesca coming along behind him.

They rode up to the fifth floor and the superintendent showed them where the men's room was. Then Parker said,

"All right. What we want you to do is go down and turn off the water. You got a watch with a second hand?"

The superintendent was confused again, but he nodded. "Yeah. Sure."

"Okay. We want you to time it. Turn it off for exactly fifteen minutes, and then turn it back on again. You got that?"

"Fifteen minutes," said the superintendent.

"You can go a few seconds one way or the other," Parker told him, "but get it as close as you can."

"Okay," the superintendent said.

"We'll give you a couple minutes to get down there," Parker said.

The superintendent turned away, shaking his head. "You never get any sleep in this damn job," he said.

"You think you got troubles," Parker told him.

"I know," the superintendent said, walking away. "It's rough all over."

Parker and Formutesca went into the men's room. Formutesca was grinning the second the door closed. "That was beautiful," he said. "That was really beautiful."

"Don't giggle and wink when he's around," Parker said. "We're not here for fun."

Formutesca looked sheepish. "I'm sorry," he said. "You're right. It was just nervousness. I'll be better now."

"Good."

Parker went over and opened the window. Four feet away and about a foot higher than the windowsill was the rim of the museum roof. "Perfect," Parker said. "Let's have the ladder."

They slid the ladder top-first out of the window till it rested with one end on the museum roof and the other end on the windowsill. Then, while Formutesca held the ladder in place, Parker went on hands and knees across it to the museum roof. He stepped off on to the roof and Formutesca pulled the ladder back in at the other end. If the super-

70

intendent should come back in while Parker was gone, Formutesca would just lean against the wall and be stupid.

The roof surface was tar, quiet beneath Parker's feet. He hurried over to the mounded shape of the elevator-shaft housing, found the padlock holding the lid down, and took from an inside pocket a small envelope with a dozen keys inside. He tried three keys before finding the right one, then put the rest back in the envelope and the envelope back in his pocket. The right key he put in a different pocket, removed the padlock, and lifted the housing cover. He got out a pencil flash and looked inside the shaft.

It was fine. There was a broad metal beam one could stand on when one first climbed in, and the side cables were easily accessible for climbing down. The top of the elevator was a bare seven feet below him now, being stopped at the top floor, which was unexpected good luck. They'd assumed the Kasempas would keep the elevator at the first-floor level when they weren't using it, in case Gonor or someone else should visit the place, but apparently they were feeling very secure and sure of themselves.

The elevator roof itself was perfect, mostly flat, metal, with the trapdoor into the elevator off toward a corner. The thing should work.

Parker put the pencil flash away, shut the cover, and put the padlock back on. Then he went back across the roof to the lighted men's room window and saw Formutesca in there looking for him.

Formutesca smiled and waved when he saw him, then pushed the ladder out the window again. Parker reached for it, rested the top end on the roof rim, and went hands and knees back to the other building.

Formutesca helped him through the window and then pulled the ladder back in and shut the window. He turned to Parker, not bothering to hide his excitement. "Well? How is it?"

"Fine," Parker said. "It'll work. How long's it been?"

Formutesca looked at his watch. "Just about eleven minutes."

"Good," Parker said. "We have time to make a mess."

For the next five minutes they attempted to make the room look like a place where plumbers had been at work. Parker flushed the three toilets, emptying their water tanks, and smeared a few streaks of grease here and there on walls and fixtures while Formutesca chipped three tiles out of the wall above one of the sinks and then carelessly glued them back on again, grouting somewhat sloppily around their edges.

When the superintendent came back, the room looked right. He looked around and said, "You got it done?"

"We think so," Parker said. "We'll have to take a look in the basement, that's all. You don't have to stay with us any more if you don't want."

"I don't know," the superintendent said. "Maybe I better."

"It's up to you," Parker said. He took Hoskins' notebook out of his pocket. "In case this thing acts up again," he said, "do me a favor. Don't call the department, call me personally. Otherwise they'll have me running my ass off. Will you do that?"

"Sure," the superintendent said. "No skin off my nose."

"Thanks," Parker said. He wrote on a page of the notebook *Mr Lynch*, EL5-2598. That was a number in Gonor's apartment. If in the next few days the superintendent began to have questions or suspicions, if he was troubled or unhappy in any way, he would now call Parker rather than anyone else. It was a way to guard against surprises when they came back.

Parker tore the page out of the notebook and gave it to the superintendent, who looked at it and tucked it away in his pants pocket. Then the three of them took the elevator down to the basement, Formutesca again carrying the ladder and toolbox. This time Formutesca stayed in character.

In the basement, Parker kept the superintendent busy

72

showing him where things were — the fuse boxes, the hot water line, the main water line — while Formutesca quietly looked around for an entrance. Parker wrote things on his clipboard, asked questions, and when Formutesca wandered over again, looked sleepy and stupid, Parker said to the superintendent, "All right, that should do it. I don't want any more trouble if I can help it."

"I know what you mean," the superintndent said, and led the way to the elevator. Behind him, Formutesca shook his head at Parker, meaning there was no usable way in.

They rode up to the first floor, walked down toward the door, and Parker stopped and said, "That valve under the sink."

The superintendent said, "What?" He was obviously thinking most about going back to bed.

Parker said to Formutesca, "You know the one I mean. Go on up and check it."

"Yeah," said Formutesca, the word full of boredom and stupidity.

"This won't take long," Parker told the superintendent. "You just take him up and let him check that valve."

"Ain't you coming?"

"I never want to see that john again," Parker said, "as long as I live."

"I feel the same way myself," the superintendent said. He was beginning to feel peevish and put-upon. He turned away unhappily and led Formutesca back to the elevator.

As soon as the elevator started upstairs, Parker went to the front door, opened it, studied the lock for a minute, and then took a ring with half a dozen keys on it from his pocket. He frowned over the keys, selected one, put it in the lock, and it worked. Satisfied, he put it away again and shut the door.

It was good he had one that would work, since the superintendent's patience was obviously beginning to run thin. If he hadn't been able to see a quiet way to get through this door he'd have had to make the superintendent show them the rear of the building next. He didn't mind exasperating the superintendent, but he didn't want the man calling some city department of water supply or something tomorrow to complain about being dragged out of bed in the middle of the night.

He waited about three minutes, and then the elevator came back down and Formutesca and the superintendent came out. Parker said, "Was it okay?" That phrasing meant things were all right down here. If the door had proved a problem, he would have said, "Was anything wrong?"

Formutesca was obviously glad to hear they were done playing this game. "Sure it was okay," he said, trying for the sullen and stupid sound again but this time not being completely successful at it.

But it wasn't a big enough slip for the superintendent to notice. His eyes were half closed; in spirit he was already back in bed and asleep. He walked Parker and Formutesca to the door, held it for them, nodded heavily when Parker voiced the hope that there wouldn't be any more trouble now, and then shut the door and went away.

Out on the sidewalk, Formutesca permitted himself a nervous grin. "That last part was scary," he said. "Being on my own with him."

"It was worth it," Parker told him.

7

They looked like small bowling pins with clock faces on their undersides. Parker held them both in his hands, looking at the clock faces, and said, "How accurate are they?"

"To the minute," Gonor said, as proud of them as if he'd manufactured them himself. He pointed to one of the clocks. "You see, you set both those red hands, that one for the hour and that one for the minute. The black hands keep the time, and when they coincide with the red hands it goes off."

They were in Gonor's war room, their arsenal spread out on the table for Parker's inspection. Pistols, machine guns, smoke bombs, gas bombs. Plus coils of rope, knives, rubber gloves, rolls of adhesive tape. And the two time bombs in Parker's hands.

Parker said, "Good. We'll go put them in place." He turned to Manado and Formutesca standing to one side. "You two all set?"

Manado was obviously frightened with something more than stage fright, but it didn't look as though it would immobilize him. He nodded jerkily, his eyes a little too wide. Formutesca, cocky now since his foray with Parker, grinned and said, "It's in the bag."

"It's never in the bag," Parker told him, "until afterwards." He turned back to Gonor. "You ready?"

"Yes." Gonor picked up two attaché cases from the floor and put them on the table. They were exactly alike, both black with brass locks. "This is yours," Gonor said, pushing one of the cases toward Parker. "Do you want to take it now or come back for it?"

75

"I'll take it now."

Gonor opened the other attaché case and put the two time bombs in it. He shut it, then looked at the other case and questioningly at Parker. "Aren't you going to count it?"

"It's all there," Parker said. "You ready?"

"Yes."

Parker took his case and left the room, Gonor following him. The other two stayed behind.

Parker and Gonor walked through the apartment in silence, went out to the elevator, rode it down, went out to Fifth Avenue, and got themselves a cab heading downtown.

"Thirty-eighth Street between Park and Lexington," Gonor said.

It was drizzling slightly, a cold March rain, the air full of clamminess. The cabby had a balled-up rag on the seat beside him, and every block or two he used it to clear condensation from the windshield. He had the wipers on slow, and they clicked back and forth with abrupt starts and slow sweeps across the glass.

They got out in front of the museum, knowing the Kasempas would be watching them from windows on the upper floors. But what would they see? Gonor, in the middle of the afternoon, unsuspectingly bringing another American scholar around to the museum.

Gonor unlocked the front door and led the way in. The air inside had the smell of an empty building, dry and chill and dusty. Shields hung on the walls in the foyer, and through doorways to the left and right Parker could see rows of glass-topped display cases. The wooden floor was highly polished and bare of rugs.

Gonor led the way: straight ahead and through a long narrow room with display cases on the left and wooden statuettes on pedestals on the right. At the far end was a doorway to a small square room with paintings on the side walls. Opposite was the elevator.

It was on the first floor now. They boarded, and as they

rode up to three Parker checked the trap-door in the ceiling. There was a small handle that had to be turned. Parker left it in the "open" position.

The elevator reached the third floor, and for the next ten minutes they looked at the exhibits there. They had no way of knowing if one of the Kasempa brothers was close enough to hear them, so they spoke seldom, and everything they did say they phrased as though Parker were a visiting professor from some college, here for research purposes.

When they went back down to the first floor, they kept up the act. In the half-hour they spent downstairs they set the two time bombs and planted them in places where they would be least likely to start fires. They were set to go off two minutes apart.

Finally, Parker said, "Thank you, Mr Gonor. It's all been very helpful to me."

"Thank you," Gonor said. "I'm glad it has been." He sounded exactly like a man trying not to show boredom.

They left the building together, Gonor carefully locking the front door, and walked up to Park Avenue, where Gonor waved and said, "There's a cab."

"I'll take the next one," Parker said.

Gonor looked at him in surprise. "Aren't you coming back with me?"

"There's no need to."

"We'd assumed—" Gonor was at a loss. "We thought you'd be coming back."

"There's nothing more to say," Parker said. "They know what to do, they know how to do it."

The cab Gonor had waved to was waiting beside them. "This is so abrupt," he said.

"We're finished," Parker said. "All you have to remember for yourself is don't leave the truck. And if something goes wrong and you have to start again, call me through Handy McKay."

"All right," said Gonor. "Well . . . thank you."

"That's all right," Parker said. He saw another cab coming up Park, and he waved to it. "Good luck," he said.

"Thank you." Gonor suddenly stuck his hand out, as though breaking a promise to himself. "It's been a pleasure," he said.

Parker took his hand. "I hope you make out," he said.

They got into their separate cabs. Parker said to the driver, "Winchester Hotel, West Forty-fourth Street." Then he sat back and watched the world outside the cab window and stopped thinking about Gonor and the diamonds and the museum.

He thought about Claire. What name was she using? Mrs Carol Bowen. At Herridge House, in Boston. In the last few days, while working out the details of this one, he hadn't thought of Claire at all, but suddenly his mind was full of her.

He could take the air shuttle; he could be with her in less than two hours.

At the hotel, he paused by the desk to tell them to get his bill ready. Then he went upstairs and into his room, and number one was there again, standing by the window watching the drizzle. The ex-colonist, the one who'd been going through Parker's suitcase way back at the beginning of this.

His two friends weren't around. In their place he held a Colt automatic casually in his right hand as though he knew how to use it but was sure it wouldn't be necessary.

Parker said, "What now?"

"I thought we could have a talk," he said.

Parker remembered the three names in Hoskins' notebook. "Which one are you?" he said. "Daask?"

He seemed surprised. "You know the names? Oh, from Hoskins, of course. No, I'm Marten, Aaron Marten."

"All right, Marten," Parker said. "What do you want to talk about?"

"We could talk about Gonor," Marten said. "When will the robbery take place? Where are the diamonds now? Where will he take them after the robbery?"

Parker shook his head. "You've got to know better," he said.

Marten seemed unruffled. "You don't want to talk about that? Very well. Would you care to talk about Mrs Carol Bowen instead? Who is no longer at Herridge House in Boston, Massachusetts?"

Three

1

Claire's head hurt. That's what woke her up, the pounding of it behind her forehead, up behind her eyes. A real killer of a headache, so that her first conscious thought was *I must have drunk too much*. But then through the pain came more consciousness, and awareness, and memory, and she thought, *I didn't drink anything yesterday*. That made her open her eyes, and she saw she was in a place she'd never been before.

She wasn't frightened at first, just bewildered. Continuing to lie there on her side, head cradled by the pillow, covers pulled up around her neck, she looked at the slice of room she could see, the gray wall and the brown kitchen chair and the closed old-fashioned-looking door, and she wondered, *Where am I?*

Her clothing was on. She suddenly realized that. She was in bed with the covers pulled up, but underneath the covers she was fully dressed. She was wearing everything but shoes.

She sat up abruptly and looked around, and it was a room she didn't know, a large bedroom with old furniture in it: the brass double bed she was in, two dressers, a vanity, night tables, and two more brown kitchen chairs. The bedside lamps had pleated pink shades. The windows had white curtains and dark green shades, the shades halfway down. Gray-white daylight poured through the lower half of the windows. Two windows, both along the wall opposite the bed.

There was no one else in the room. Claire listened, and there was no sound from anywhere in the house.

Where was she? How had she gotten here?

It was hard to think with this pounding headache, hard to

make sense out of anything. She bent her head and massaged her temples, and that seeemed to work a little. She continued to massage gently and tried to think.

Where had she been last night? Where had she been at all yesterday?

She'd gone to a beauty parlor yesterday afternoon, downtown on Franklin Street, she remembered that. And then she'd gone looking to buy a fall, but she couldn't find anything she really liked that matched her hair color. She'd gone back to the hotel, hoping Parker would be there today — it was nine days today — or at least a message from him, but there had been nothing. She hadn't felt like dinner alone in a restaurant so she'd ordered something from room service, and while she'd eaten she'd looked at the paper to see what movie she wanted to sit through tonight or if there was anything at all bearable on television.

Had she gone to a movie? She couldn't remember any movie, couldn't remember any television either. What had she done after dinner? The last thing she could remember was eating dinner sitting on the chair at the writing-desk, the dishes spread out on the desk, the paper propped up against the wall in front of her. And feeling tired. And waking up here.

Drugged? Could that be the reason for this headache and the vagueness of her memory of last night? It had been a different waiter who'd brought in her dinner, but that hadn't meant anything at the time; there were several different waiters she'd seen in the last nine days.

But that was what it must hae been. She could remember eating dinner, not noticing any odd tastes about anything, and then growing very sleepy. Sitting at the writing-desk, the dishes in front of her, food left uneaten and she growing sleepier and sleepier.

Had she gotten up from the desk and gone over to stretch out on the bed? She couldn't remember exactly. It seemed as though she'd done that, or at least had wanted to do it, but she couldn't remember whether or not she'd actually made it out of the chair and over to the bed.

She rubbed her head. If only the pain would stop. She couldn't think; she couldn't concentrate.

Who would do this?

She looked at her watch. It was still running and it showed twenty-five minutes past four. Past four? It must be afternoon; she must have been asleep nearly twenty hours.

She pushed the covers off and slowly put her legs over the side of the bed. She was very shaky, nerves all ajangle. The pain in her head was worse when she moved, so she moved slowly, gingerly. Also, she didn't want anyone to hear her and know she was awake. If there was anyone around to hear.

Standing made her dizzy. She kept one hand on the wall and tiptoed in stocking feet over to the door. It was locked. Gently she turned the knob, easily she pulled, and the door was locked.

The windows? She took the long way around, always keeping next to the wall, one palm flat on the wall for support. She reached the first window, remained leaning against the wall beside it, and bent her head to the glass to look out.

Second floor. A lake, with partially thawing ice, looking very cold and very bleak. Mountains beyond the lake, also cold, also bleak. A scruffy brown yard between the house and the lake, with a few bare-branched trees and some woody bushes. A dark, squat boathouse, and beside it a concrete deck.

A key grated in the door behind her and she spun around, suddenly terrified, losing her balance and almost falling, but leaning against the wall instead. Staying there beside the window, she watched the door open and a man come in.

It didn't surprise her that he was one of the three who had been at the beginning of all this, before Gonor had shown up.

He looked at her and said, "You're awake. Good." Then

he frowned, studying her across the room. "Something wrong?"

She shook her head. She couldn't find anything to say, and she was terrified of what he might do.

He kept frowning, standing just inside the door, and then he seemed all at once to understand and to be made strangely embarrassed by it. He spread his hands, palms down. "You're all right here," he said. "You're safe here. Do you want something to eat?"

She shook her head again. Her fear was beginning to fade, not so much because of his assurances as his embarrassment, but there was still nothing to say to him.

He looked around, apparently at a loss, wanting to establish contact and not knowing how. "If you need anything," he said, "just knock on the door. I'll come by."

"I need to go home," she said. "Back to the hotel."

"I'm sorry," he said. "Not yet."

"When?"

"Pretty soon. You sure you're not hungry?"

She surprised herself by asking, "Do you have any aspirin?"

He smiled happily. "Sure," he said. "Be right back." He left, and she noticed he took the time to lock the door behind him.

Now she was angry at herself for having asked. It had given him the contact he wanted; it had given him her acceptance of the situation. She felt as though she had allowed him a victory he didn't deserve, and she considered refusing the aspirin when he brought it, but realized that would be an empty gesture and wouldn't reclaim the loss.

What a stupid way to be thinking. She looked around the room, cold and bare and minimal.

She needed Parker.

2

Jock Daask liked his women with meat on their bones and brains in their heads, and this girl Claire had both. He sat across the kitchen table from her, watching her eat the corn flakes and milk that was the only food they had for her, and he reflected that he would have liked to have met her some other way. He reflected also on the sexual implications of their current roles in relation to one another — kidnapper and victim — but the possibilities for rape didn't really interest him. Jock Daask wasn't that sort of man.

He wasn't all that sure what sort of man he was, in fact. His current roles could only be described in negatives — he had kidnapped but was not a kidnapper, he would steal but was not a thief — and it seemed to him his whole life was expressed only in the same terms of contradiction. He had been born in Africa, but was not an African. His parents were Europeans, but he was not a European. He had done well at the university in England, but he was not an intellectual. He had been a mercenary soldier in various parts of Africa, but he was not a rootless adventurer. There was nothing about him, it seemed, that did not include its own negative.

Jock Daask was the son of a wealthy plantation owner in Africa, and he had grown up always knowing that everything and everybody he saw belonged to his father and would one day belong to him. His friends in his youth were the children of other white landowners, and even then they had all seemed to be aware of their essential dislocation, at once the ruling class and exiles. Still, it was worth exile to be a member of the ruling class.

Until independence. The nation of Dhaba was spared the

87

more gruesome birth pains of many of the new African states, but even in a land of peaceful turnover one fact could not be gotten around: the white ruling class had to go.

Daask had been in London at the time, doing postgraduate work at the university, and he hadn't known anything was wrong until his father phoned him from London Airport to come out and pick him up. Their land had been taken from them, not by spear-waving cannibals but by paper-waving bureaucrats, bland men with empty smiles.

The number of ex-colonists in London and in other parts of Europe continued to grow. And the idea of counterattack grew, from men like Aaron Marten, whom Daask had known since childhood, who were determined to get their own back one way or another no matter what. And from men like General Enfehr Goma, the unsuccessful first candidate for president of Dhaba, who would be willing to live the life of a comfortable figurehead if the Aaron Martens could put them on the throne.

They could do it. There was nothing strategic about Dhaba, not in minerals or geographic location or rivers or anything else, and so no European power would intervene. The neighboring African states all had sufficient internal problems to keep them from doing anything more than complain at the UN. All they needed was the money to mount the offensive. The current president, Colonel Joseph Lubudi, was so patently corrupt that the masses of the nation might even welcome General Goma, or at least wouldn't be violently opposed to him.

But it couldn't be done without money. And from where would the money come? The ex-landowners had lost practically everything. General Goma had no money of his own and couldn't attract the support of anyone with money. So where would they get the money?

From Dhaba. From Colonel Lubudi. From the Colonel's brother-in-law, Patrick Kasempa.

Daask again looked at the woman Claire eating a third

bowl of cereal. If he were Parker, and this Claire were his woman, he would trade Gonor and the diamonds for her in a minute. Parker would cooperate; Daask was sure of it.

She became aware of his eyes on her and abruptly stopped eating. "That's all I want," she said sullenly, pushing the bowl away.

"You must still be hungry," he said, trying to sound gentle and friendly. He knew it was absurd, but he wanted her not to dislike him.

And it was true that she had to still be hungry. She hadn't eaten since the drugged dinner at the hotel in Boston last night at around seven o'clock, and here it was nearly midnight. Twenty-nine hours without food. Bob had insisted they not offer her anything to eat until she asked for it, so all she had had at first was the aspirin and water he'd brought her this afternoon. When she'd finally knocked on the door and asked for something to eat it was clear she hadn't wanted to ask for anything at all but had been driven to it by hunger.

And something in his expression when she'd met his eyes just now had driven her away from hunger again. "I don't want any more," she said and folded her arms as though she were chilly, though it was warm here in the kitchen.

Bob Quilp was out in the living-room waiting for the call from Aaron saying that Parker would cooperate, that everything was going to be all right. Daask had a very strong feeling about the closeness of this kitchen, his solitude with this woman, the persistent sexual overtones of the relationship thrust upon them. He couldn't help it, and he didn't intend to do anything about it, but the aura itself was pleasurable and he wanted to prolong it.

"A glass of milk," he said. "Would you like that?"

"I want to go upstairs again," she said. She got to her feet and stood there waiting.

Daask was suddenly irritated by her. Didn't she feel the ambience between them? Wasn't she aware of what sort of person he *could* be, how lucky she was that he was gentle? He wanted to say something about it, to point it out to her, but he couldn't find any phrasing that didn't sound silly somehow. Or threatening.

He shrugged and got to his feet. "Up to you," he said. "You go first."

They went up to the second floor, and she went willingly into her room. He stood in the doorway a minute, watching her go over to the bed and sit down with her back to him.

Then he said, "In a little while we'll have to tie you up."

She turned her head, and it pleased him to see a little glint of fear in her eyes. "Why? I won't try to get away."

"We'll be leaving," he said. "We'll tie you when we go. But we're going to tell Parker where you are, so don't worry. He'll probably be here before morning."

She shook her head. "He won't do what you want him to do."

"Of course he will," Daask said reasonably. "You're more important to him than Gonor is; it only makes sense."

"He can't stand to be pushed," she said.

"He'll cooperate," Daask said. "It's only sensible."

She shrugged and turned her back again.

Daask was about to say something else, but from downstairs he heard the ringing of a telephone. "That's it now," he said and shut the door. He locked it and hurried back downstairs.

3

William Manado sat on the floor in the back of the truck and fingered his machine gun. It was too dark to see anything except when an occasional automobile drove down Thirty-eighth Street from Park Avenue and its headlights shone through the windows in the rear doors, illuminating himself and Formutesca sitting across the way. Formutesca smiled encouragingly at him every time there was light that way, but in the intervals of darkness there was no encouragement from anywhere, and Manado was frightened.

He hadn't shown it; not to Formutesca, not to Parker, certainly not to Gonor. He hadn't shown it, he wouldn't show it, and he wouldn't let it interfere. But he couldn't deny it either — he was afraid.

Unlike Formutesca and Gonor, unlike most of the governing class of Dhaba, Manado was not from a professional family. There were no doctors, lawyers, civil servants or engineers in his background. He had come from a village family, a very poor village family, and he would be a very poor villager himself today if it were not for one thing. Manado could run.

He was fast, and he was tireless, and he could pace himself. He had run himself on to the track team at Tchidanga School, and he had run himself into an exchange scholarship for a Midwestern American university. Fortunately, his brain was as fast as his body, and he'd been able to take advantage of the advantages his running had brought him. He majored in political science at the American university, mostly because all exchange students were expected to major in political science, and took his minor in mathematics, because he liked to watch numbers run. As for America, what that country offered him because he had brains and speed baffled him almost as much as what was refused him because he was black. Afterwards, when people at home asked him about that, what it was like to be a black man in America, he always said, "Well, it takes some getting used to." What he meant was, "I'm not sure, but I think maybe it's worth getting used to."

His experience of the United States got him offered the post at the UN mission, and the ambivalence of his feelings toward the United States made him accept. Would it be different in New York City from in the Midwest? Would it be different for a member of a UN mission rather than a student? Not much.

In a way, it was America's ambivalence toward him that first made him consciously a patriot about his homeland. He saw that Dhaba with idealistic men at her helm could eventually offer everything America offers, and without the left-handed taking away. He wanted that; he wanted it badly.

Badly enough to be sitting here in this darkness, a machine gun cradled in his lap, waiting to steal and to kill.

Could he kill? He hated the Kasempas for their rape of his homeland. He was afraid of them for their reputations as brutal men. What the hatred and the fear would combine to form he didn't yet know. He had never killed anyone, had rarely ever fought with anyone. He had a secret admiration for men like Parker, who could face the bloodiest possiblities without flinching, but he believed he could never be like them.

He heard movement, a rustling sound, and knew it was Formutesca looking at his watch again, reading the green fingers of the luminous dial. Then Formutesca whispered, "Two o'clock."

Time. Manado nodded, even though Formutesca couldn't see him, and moved on hands and knees to the rear of the truck dragging his machine gun behind him. He looked out

92

the window in the door and the street was empty, so he pushed the door open and climbed out to the street, leaving the machine gun on the floor of the truck.

Formutesca climbed out after him. "Start unloading," he said and went around to talk to Gonor in the cab of the truck.

Manado brought out the ladder and propped it against the rear of the truck. Then he got his own machine gun, found Formutesca's, and wrapped them both in an old pink bedspread and laid the package on the curb. Finally he took out the long wooden toolkit and put that also on the curb. He shut the doors, and Formutesca came back.

"All set," Formutesca said.

Manado looked up at the museum's top-floor windows. They were dark; they'd been dark for over an hour now.

Formutesca carried the ladder; Manado carried the toolkit and guns. They crossed the curb and walked to the building next door to the museum. Formutesca had a key that would open the inner door. There was no one around.

They couldn't use the elevator; they didn't know whether the superintendent could hear the motor or not. He had seemed unusually conscientious — Parker and Formutesca had both said so — and he just might come out to see who was moving around in his building at two in the morning.

So they climbed stairs to the fifth floor, and Formutesca led the way down the hall to the men's room. He switched the light on and Manado said doubtfully, "Should we do that? What if somebody sees?"

"We can't work in the dark," Formutesca said.

"We have flashlights."

Formutesca shook his head. "Parker says people don't pay any attention to an ordinary light in a window," he said. "But they see a flashlight moving around, right away they think it's a burglar."

"I suppose so," said Manado, but the bright light continued to bother him. It made him feel exposed, as though hundreds of people were watching. Unconsciously, he moved with his shoulders hunched. Formutesca was the one who'd been through this before, so Manado allowed himself to be taught. Formutesca showed him how the ladder was placed and then said, "You go across. Take your time, and you'll be better off it you look straight ahead. I'll hold the ladder steady at this end."

"All right," said Manado.

"You going to take the guns?"

"Yes."

"Get up on the windowsill and I'll hand them to you."

Manado had no particular fear of heights, but crossing a space five stories up on a ladder was making him very nervous. He crouched on the windowsill while Formutesca handed him the package of guns, then put the package down gently crosswise on the ladder. He pushed the package ahead of himself and went crawling slowly out over the air.

In a way, he was glad this was happening at night. All he could see below him was blackness, with only the ladder itself and the roof rim ahead illuminated by spill from the window behind him. The package of guns gave him something to think about too, besides his nervousness.

He got across, lowered the package to the roof without making a clatter, got on to the roof himself, and turned around to signal to Formutesca that everything was all right.

Formutesca called softly, "Hold it steady for me."

"I will."

"One minute."

Formutesca left the window, and Manado saw him walk over to the door and switch off the light. They wouldn't be coming back this way, so Formutesca would have to cross in darkness.

Nothing happened for quite a while, and Manado understood that Formutesca was waiting for his eyes to adjust. Manado stood leaning on the end of the ladder holding it steady and waited. Now that the light was out, now that he

94

was safely across the emptiness, he felt much better. The darkness cloaked him. His presence on this roof meant the enemy's stronghold was already breached. Manado was beginning to feel good.

A small clatter, and vibration of the ladder against his hands. Peering across there, he saw that Formutesca had placed the toolkit on the ladder. Now here he came, pushing the heavy box ahead of him, moving slowly.

When the toolkit was close enough, Manado took one hand from the ladder and lifted it over on to the roof. Then he helped Formutesca over the edge, and the two of them pulled the ladder over and laid it down on the roof. They had to leave the window open over there; they had no choice, but it shouldn't matter.

The day's drizzle had ended several hours ago, but the air was cold enough so that a wet, slushy slickness covered most of the roof. They had to walk carefully carrying their equipment, and Manado wondered what would happen if he lost his balance and fell, the machine guns crashing around.

But it didn't happen. They got to the elevator housing, and Formutesca used the key to unlock it. Now they did use a flashlight, seeing that the interior was as Parker had described it. The elevator was just below them on the fourth floor. Apparently, the Kasempas kept it on the first floor during the day for security's sake but didn't bother about doing that at night.

In the toolkit was a coil of rope. While Manado got it out, Formutesca climbed inside the elevator housing and stood spraddlelegged on the metal beams in there. Manado handed the rope in to him, and Formutesca tied one end to the central beam, being sure it was on tight and secure. The other end he lowered on to the elevator top, where it lay looped like a brown snake. They'd brought enough to reach the first floor, just in case.

While Formutesca climbed back out of the housing, Manado was getting the gloves from the toolkit. They worked now in silence, having gone over the details of this time and again with Parker. They both knew their parts.

Manado handed Formutesca a pair of gloves and put on the other pair himself. Then he climbed in where Formutesca had been. Their flashlight had a magnet on the side and was now attached to the housing, pointing down. In its light, Manado grabbed the rope and lowered himself slowly to the top of the elevator.

It made a metallic *pop* when he stood on it, like a cooling oven, not loud, but startling in the middle of silence. Manado froze, one hand still on the rope, and listened. But there was no more sound, and when he looked up, Formutesca already had the other rope around the package of guns and was lowering it to him.

Manado eased the package down and untied the rope. As Formutesca pulled the rope back up, Manado opened the bedspread, smoothing it out over a large area of the elevator roof. It would muffle any more sounds they might make and it would keep them from getting filthy from the years of accumulated dust up here. He left the trapdoor area clear, and he put the two machine guns out of the way to one side.

The toolkit came down next. Manado got it, set it on the bedspread, and then gathered in the rope as Formutesca dropped it to him. He rolled the rope into a ball while Formutesca slid down the other one. Light and shadows flickered crazily for a minute, since Formutesca was bringing the flashlight down with him, and when Manado looked up he felt one sudden instant of irrational and superstitious fear. Like himself, Formutesca was dressed entirely in black, shoes and trousers and mackinaw and gloves, and sliding down the rope there, the flashlight beam bouncing this way and that, he looked absolutely satanic, lithe and lean and dangerous.

Manado felt the instant fear, and then he thought, *That's what I look like too,* and all at once he felt very good. Not afraid of anything.

96

Standing beside him, Formutesca looked at his watch and whispered, "Ten after. Not bad."

Manado was grinning. "I'm ready to go right now," he whispered.

Formutesca grinned back at him. "I know what you mean. It's too bad we have to wait." He looked around. "Well, we might as well get ourselves comfortable."

Manado's grin faded slowly. Comfortable. Wait. His good feeling evaporated as fast as it had come. He looked up, the top of the housing indistinct up there now that the light source was down here. All at once it seemed as though they were in a grave.

"Sit down," whispered Formutesca, who had already done so. "I want to switch off this light."

Manado sat down, and Formutesca switched them into darkness. They had had to leave the housing open up there, and damp, cold air was settling in. Manado shivered.

4

Patrick Kasempa couldn't sleep. It was the usual thing. He sat in the small room at the rear of the top floor, what he called his insomnia room, and he played hand after hand of solitaire. He never cheated, he rarely won, and he kept track of his record on a notepad he kept just to his right on the tabletop.

He never had insomnia at home in Tchidanga, never. It was the climate that did it; he'd known that for years — the clammy climate of Europe and North America affected him badly. He always had insomnia when he traveled north from Dhaba. Only in the soft nights of the tropics could he find normal sleep.

Another two months of this. He didn't know if he could last; he wasn't sure how much longer he could take this. Joseph had made his move too early, that was obvious. He should have waited another three months before starting; he should have organized his timetable better. The result was, here they were, seven hundred thousand dollars' worth of diamonds in their possession, sitting here like monkeys in a treetop waiting for some hunter to notice them and shoot them out of the branches. It was enough to keep a man awake even if he didn't have insomnia to begin with.

The answer was, Colonel Joseph Lubudi was a stupid man. And the Colonel's sister Lucille, whom Kasempa had married out of misplaced ambition, was as stupid as her brother or they wouldn't be here now. No, the two of them would be in Acapulco at this very minute with the diamonds, rich and anonymous and safe. And asleep.

But no. They had to stay here in New York, this ugly city,

this clammy graveyard, the whole city dank and gray. It's a wonder anyone could sleep in a place like this. They had to stay here another two months; they had to wait for Lucille's stupid brother to make his stupid move, to be caught, to be torn to pieces by an enraged mob and the pieces to be buried in some potter's field somewhere. *Then* they could go to Acapulco, not before.

"Joseph will get away," Lucille kept saying. "You'll see." *Bah.*

The fact was, Colonel Lubudi would *not* get away, and Kasempa knew it. The Colonel had handled this whole affair so sloppily it was a miracle they hadn't been found out yet. Would his enemies let him out of Dhaba without first counting the governmental knives and forks? Nonsense. Joseph was a dead man, and Patrick Kasempa knew it.

But he couldn't tell that to Lucille. He could hint, he could talk around it, he could try to make her understand it herself, but if he were to directly advocate their disappearing with the diamonds, Lucille would be thrust into a dilemma of loyalties, husband versus brother, and Kasempa wasn't all that sure in his mind which way such a dilemma would be resolved.

So there was nothing to do but wait. In New York City. Sleeplessly.

Another hand was stuck. Kasempa sighed and gathered the cards together and shuffled them. His wristwatch said the time was two forty-five. The way he was feeling, with luck he might be able to get to bed and to sleep by four. He shook his head and dealt out a new hand.

There was an explosion.

Kasempa looked up, the cards in his left hand. The blackness outside the window was unchanged.

It had been near, very near. In the building?

The alarm hadn't sounded, so it couldn't be either the front or back door. When the building had been converted to a museum and this apartment put in for the full-time curator the place had never needed, an alarm system had been built in to help protect the place from burglaries at night. When switched on, the alarm rang a bell in the master bedroom if either door was tampered with or opened. They kept the alarm switched on at all times, and the only instances when it had rung were the two times Gonor had brought visitors to the museum, once a few weeks ago and then again just this afternoon. If the explosion had meant someone trying to break in through one of the doors, the alarm would have sounded. So if it was in the building it had to be something else.

What?

Kasempa put the cards down, and got to his feet. He went to the door, opened it, and stood in the hallway listening.

Nothing.

A door along the hall opened, and Kasempa's brother Albert appeared, sleepy-eyed but with a pistol in his hand. "What was it?"

"I don't know. Listen."

The two brothers stood facing one another listening. All the brothers were physically alike, short and bull-like and broad, but faster-moving than they looked.

Another. A sudden loud blast, an explosion. Like a hand grenade going off, or something larger.

In the building.

Albert said, "What the hell? It's downstairs!"

"Come on!"

Another door opened as they hurried toward the elevator, and their brother Ralph called, "What's going on?"

"Stay here," Kasempa shouted back. "We'll take a look downstairs."

The elevator was already on this floor, and the door slid back when Kasempa pressed the button. They went in together and Albert said, "All the way down?"

"Of course!"

Albert pushed the button for the first floor, the door slid

shut, and they started down.

Kasempa heard the slight sound above him. He looked up, and a rectangular opening was spreading in the ceiling. He saw eyes, hands in darkness, and something was flung in.

A grenade!

"No!" he shouted, recoiling. The elevator was suddenly too small. He and Albert were cramped together; neither could move.

But the thing hit the floor without exploding. It seemed to fall apart, to break open in two halves. A faint yellowish mist rose up.

Albert was shouting, Kasempa couldn't tell what. But he knew what that was; he knew it was gas; he knew he'd been mousetrapped and he was a dead man. He knew it, but he refused to let it be so. He pushed savagely past his brother, reaching for the buttons. He wouldn't breathe; he refused to breathe, though he had already inhaled some of it in the first few seconds after it broke open. Albert was falling over, falling into his path, his weight leaning on Kasempa's chest. Kasempa gritted his teeth, pushed the heavy weight away, and got his fingers on the buttons.

If he could stop the elevator. If he could get the doors open. If he could get *out* of here.

He could feel the nausea welling up, feel the darkness behind it. He could feel his strength draining away. He leaned on his fingers, pressing all the buttons.

The elevator was stopping. Green kaleidoscopes were irising in around the edges of his vision. Albert had slid to the floor, his weight now leaning against Kasempa's legs, and the strength was rushing like blood out of his legs.

The door slid open. He saw it sliding, as slow as eternity, with the last of his vision, saw the second-floor displays in semidarkness, saw the green kaleidoscope iris close over his eyes, felt his hands sliding down the smooth wall of the elevator. He tried to take a step, out and away, but all that happened was that his knee bent. It kept bending.

101

5

Formutesca continued to sit on the trapdoor after the elevator had stopped. He could hear the door slide open. He sat there listening, controlling himself, feeling the excitement and nevousness in him like low-voltage electricity pouring through his body. Across the way, Manado sat and stared at him. But Formutesca had no time now to think about Manado or to worry about whether or not Manado would carry his weight when the time came. He had no time now to think about what was or was not happening in the elevator, no time to think about the fact that no attempt at all had been made to push the trapdoor up. All he could think about was what was happening inside himself.

Bara Formutesca was African middle class, and he himself wasn't entirely sure what that meant. His father was a British-trained doctor, his mother a German-trained schoolteacher, and their son was an American-trained diplomat. But what did that mean, or matter?

When he was very young, six or seven, Formutesca first learned about the two words white men in his country used when referring to black men. One was a word that meant *monkey*, and that referred to the tribesmen outside the cities and the workers on the big estates and the urban poor. And the other was a word that meant something like *civilized* and something like *evolved*, and that referred to the white-collar workers and the professional men, all the Africans who had received training in European skills and who conducted their lives by European standards. In the way it was used, this second word seemed to imply also a further level of meaning, something slyly contemptible, something like *castrated* or *tamed.* It had seemed to Formutesca, as a very young child hearing those words, that between the two it was better to be a monkey than a eunuch, and ever since then he had watched himself for traces of that wildness and that brash humor that he thought of as being the essence of monkeyness.

But his parentage, his background and his training all made him tend in the other direction toward the tamed. He was too intelligent to throw all that over — the average "monkey" in Dhaba had an annual income of one hundred forty-seven dollars and would die of one of several possible dreadful diseases before his fortieth birhday. But when he saw the bland, emasculated Africans in their blue-gray suits gliding along the halls at the UN as though on muffled roller-skates, he determined over and over again never to let that — *depersonalization* was what it was — happen to him.

Could one of them possibly be here now in his place? One of those smooth-faced amiable pets? Never.

In the dim light he saw Manado's eyes gleaming, and he suddenly smiled because it occurred to him that he and Manado were both exceptions to the rule, and for opposite reasons. Manado was a monkey trying to be a mannequin, and Formutesca was a mannequin trying to be a monkey.

Manado whispered, "What's that sound?"

Formutesca had heard it too. A click, and then a thudding sound, and then more clicks, and then silence. He held up his hand for Manado to be quiet and listened. Nothing happened for half a minute and then the sequence started again: the click, the thud, more clicks, silence.

"The elevator," Formutesca said. he didn't bother to whisper, and his words had a slight echo up and down the elevator shaft. He made hand motions, bringing the sides of his hands together to illustrate what he meant. "The doors are trying to close."

Manado said, "What's the matter with them?" There was something trembling in his voice.

There was very little light here. Formutesca switched on

the flashlight and shone it on Manado's face. Manado's eyes were wide with barely controlled panic, his mouth hung open, and his whole manner was startled, on the verge of flight. He seemed to be wearing hysteria like a plastic raincoat; he could be seen through it, but dimly.

It would be no good if Manado fell apart. It would be very dangerous for Formutesca if he couldn't rely on his second man. Quietly he said, "There's something in their way. They can't close because something is blocking them."

"What?"

Carefully, Formutesca said, "Probably a body."

Manado blinked, then shut his eyes entirely and held up a hand. "The light," he said.

"Sorry." Formutesca switched it off. "Shall we go see?"

Manado didn't answer. Formutesca, peering at him, said, "Are you ready?"

"Yes. I nodded."

"I didn't see you."

"I'm sorry, I should have, I didn't realize."

Formutesca reached out and grabbed Manado's wrist. "Don't fall apart, William," he said. "We need each other."

"I won't. I just don't want to be up here any more."

"Neither do I."

Formutesca lifted the trapdoor, keeping his head to one side of the opening. He wanted to be sure they were both unconscious before he showed himself, and he also didn't want to be in the line of any updraft in case some of the gas was still active. He knew it was supposed to be inert by now, but he felt a kind of vague awe toward gas and didn't trust it.

Light columned upward from the opening, but that was all. Formutesca counted to three and then looked over the edge and down into the elevator.

Both. One face up along the back, the other face down across the entrance, his upper half out on to the floor, his body keeping the door from shutting again.

Formutesca turned and nodded at Manado. "Perfect," he

whispered, and was pleased to see Manado manage a smile.

Formutesca went first, dropping lithely down into the elevator and stepping over the body in the doorway. Ahead of him was a largish room full of display cases with wooden masks lined along the far wall. Monkey faces looking at him. He felt like an initiate.

He heard Manado land behind him. Not looking back, he moved farther into the semidarkness.

Manado called softly, "Just a minute."

Formutesca turned back just in time to see Manado slit the throat of the one in the elevator. The blood looked like red paint, too sudden and thin to be real.

Formutesca went blank. All he could do was stand there in shock and amazement. It was true they'd talked this over beforehand, he and Manado and Gonor, and decided the Kasempas couldn't be allowed to live. They would have to be killed, all five people in the building, and their bodies buried in the basement. They'd argued that out more than a week ago knowing it would be too dangerous to everybody concerned to leave the Kasempas alive.

Still, to have it happen so fast, so casually, just a few seconds ago he'd been worrying that Manado would panic, and now, with a calm that even Parker might envy, Manado had dropped into the elevator and methodically slit a Kasempa's throat.

In his shock and confusion Formutesca remembered when they'd found out that Balando was the one betraying them to Goma and his white mercenaries. He remembered that it was Gonor who had finally killed Balando and it was he himself who had done most of the questioning, but it was Manado who had suggested the tortures. They hadn't had to use them; the suggestions had been enough. Manado, serious-looking, studious, studying Balando with efficient earnestness, suggesting horrors he'd heard of when he was a child.

Suddenly Formutesca knew just how many light-years he was from monkeydom. However much he might play at savagery he was a tame lamb, nothing but a tame lamb.

Cast adrift, he invoked Parker. How would Parker act now? How would that man think? What would he be? Neither monkey nor lamb, but something better than both. It seemed to Formutesca that Parker would remain cold, aloof, emotionless, that he would be like a computer, quickly but methodically solving the problem of this robbery, moving through it like a pre-programmed robot. That's how he must be himself if he was going to survive. This was not a joke.

Manado was saying something. Formutesca looked at him, trying to understand, and saw Manado gesture with the streaked knife at the other unconscious man, the one across the doorway.

Formutesca shook his head, forcing himself to move. "No," he said. "He's mine. Get the guns."

Manado nodded and stooped to wipe the knife blade on the dead man's shirt.

Formutesca's own knife was in a sheath attached to his belt and tucked into his right hip pocket He had felt good putting it on, felt like a commando.

He'd never killed anyone in his life.

The knife handle felt bulky and awkward in his hand. He went to one knee beside the Kasempa and then he saw he would have to turn the man over first. He put the knife on the floor, grabbed the unconscious man's shoulder and belt, and heaved him over. He was heavy and he would go only half-way, his hips then resting against the edge of the elevator doorway where the doors were recessed. Every thirty seconds the doors tried to close, recoiling when the rubber leading edge struck the body.

Formutesca left the body lying on its side. He picked up his knife again, and with his other hand pushed back on the Kasempa's forehead exposing his throat. He kept thinking, *I can't make a botch of this; I have to do it right the first time; I won't be able to do it twice.*

106

He held the knife against the throat. He could hear the man's breathing; it sounded as though he had sinus trouble. He knew Manado was back up on top of the elevator again waiting to hand down the machine guns.

If only they could have gotten lethal gas. Gas murdered so much more cleanly.

Formutesca dragged the knife across the throat. It was very sharp, but in his desperation not to have to do it more than once he pressed as though it were dull. Blood spurted out as though he'd discovered oil, and he jumped back. It was on his trouser leg, his sleeve, his hand.

He looked at himself, looked at the knife, looked at the body. There was no more sinus breathing.

Shakily, Formutesca smiled. *I did it*, he thought. He wanted to say it aloud, but he resisted. He felt no more fear, no more revulsion. It was accomplished, and everything after this would be routine. He felt vast relief and a great deal of pride.

Now he knew what army men were talking about when they mentioned the baptism of fire.

Because he'd cut so deep there had been much more welling up of blood than with Manado. It was hard to get his knife clean; the handle was also smeared. He did what he could, wiped his hand on his corpse's trouser leg, then put away the knife and went back into the elevator.

Manado's face in the ceiling opening was the face of a brother. Formutesca smiled up at him and saw the surprise with which Manado smiled back. Then Manado lowered the guns to him and dropped back down again. Formutesca handed him one of the guns and led the way out of the elevator.

The stairs were in the middle of the building. They turned on no lights, the spill from the elevator giving them enough vague illumination as far as the staircase. From here on they would prefer darkness.

They were closer than they'd planned, the elevator having

stopped on the second floor. They moved slowly enough to be silent.

As Formutesca was about to start up the stairs Manado touched his arm. Formutesca looked at him questioningly and Manado leaned close to whisper, "I'm all right now."

Smiling at the silliness of that, Formutesca nodded.

"It was just the waiting," Manado whispered. "But now I'll be okay."

6

Lucille Kasempa had been awake since the second explosion. She'd thrown a robe around her heavy body and come out to the hall to find her husband's brother Ralph standing there wearing nothing but trousers and a pistol. She'd said, "Where's Patrick?"

"Went downstairs with Albert."

The fourth brother, Morton, had come out then wearing even less than Ralph. Only the trousers, no gun. The three of them had stood around asking each other what had happened, and finally Lucille had gone down to the elevator and pressed the button to bring it up so she could go down and see for herself what was happening, but it hadn't come.

And now she was beginning to worry. They'd been down there too long, and there wasn't a sound.

She didn't like this. She'd had a foreboding from the beginning, from the time Joseph had first come to her with his scheme for getting his money out of the country. "Why do it?" she'd asked him. "In Tchidanga you have everything. You're president of the country, you have power and prestige, you're rich. Why give it all up?"

But he'd said, "How much longer do you suppose I can hold on to this thing? If Goma doesn't get me, Indindu will. The two of them are out there, both after my head, both after this job. Goma's got the whites behind him, Indindu's got the army and the diplomatic staff behind him. It's only a matter of time — a year, maybe less than a year. I'd rather be a Faruk than a Diem."

And she was the only one he could trust. He'd said that, and she'd known it was so. But she'd left Tchidanga with a

109

heavy heart, and it wasn't just because she was giving up the life she loved, the social position, the importance of being the president's sister. It was also this sense of foreboding, this fear that the scheme wouldn't work. They were doomed; they were bringing down upon their heads a violence none of them would escape.

That was why she'd insisted on the children's going to boarding school in Scotland. She didn't want them anywhere around when it happened, if it happened.

If it was happening now.

She had always thought of the Blessed Virgin Mary as her special protector, her patron saint. She had always prayed to the Blessed Virgin. In her bedroom at home there was a small shrine to the Blessed Virgin. She had always come with all her troubles to the Blessed Virgin.

But how could she pray now? For a month that had troubled her. How could she ask the Blessed Virgin's aid and intercession now? How could she say, "Help me help my brother rob his country, betray his trust, cheat the people who gave him his high office?" How could she ask that? All she could do was say, "Blessed Virgin, although you cannot condone what I am doing, still I pray you understand why I could not refuse, and for the sake of my children help us through this hour of trouble."

Was help not to come?

She could hear nothing from downstairs. How long had it been now, ten minutes, fifteen minutes?

If only there were an intercom in this building. There certainly should be.

Maybe she would be able to hear something at the staircase. She started in that direction, and all of a sudden around the corner there she saw two men coming.

All in black.

With machine guns in their hands.

She shrieked and flung herself at the nearest door. She fell through, rolling, the door banging against the wall, and

110

heard the sudden vicious chatter of the machine guns behind her. Ralph and Morton had been farther down the hall, exposed, vulnerable.

She had never moved so fast in her life. She rolled to her feet; she grabbed the edge of the door; she slammed it. There was a latch on the inside, and she locked it, even though she knew it could only delay the inevitable for a few more seconds.

She was in Patrick's insomnia room. A game of solitaire was in progress on the table. A notepad there had obscure rows of numbers.

Patrick? He had gone downstairs. Those two men had come up from downstairs. Patrick could no longer be alive.

She shook her head, having no time to think about Patrick now, Patrick or anything else. She hurried to the window, flung it open to the cold damp air, and stuck her head out. "Help!" she cried. "Help!"

The fire escape was down to the right, three windows away. Even a circus performer wouldn't be able to get there from here.

Would no one hear her? "Help! Please, help!"

No lights went on in the row of black buildings before her. Nothing happened.

The door crashed open behind her. She spun around, flattening her back against the wall beside the window. The two men came in, and one of them stood in the middle of the room while the other one came over and shut the window. He smiled crookedly at her. "Not in New York," he said. "It is well known no one listens in New York."

He had blood on his face, on one sleeve, on the knee of his trousers. She stared at him in horror.

He continued to smile. "You have nothing to fear from us," he said. His voice was insinuating, like a seducer's. "Just tell us where the diamonds are," he said.

She shook her head. "I don't know. My husband kept them; I don't know what he did with them."

111

He stopped smiling. Mocking her, he looked troubled. As though he really worried about her, he said, "We aren't going to have to force you to tell us, are we? We don't want to have to hurt you."

She looked at the other one still in the middle of the room, his machine gun pointed at her head. He looked so young, so much more innocent than the other one. Would he stand by and let her be tortured?

He'd have to, of course. The older one must be in command here.

She wouldn't be able to stand torture, she knew that.

It was all over now, all Joseph's plans, just as she'd feared. Even if she didn't tell them, even if she let them kill her without telling them, they wouldn't have to search very hard to find the diamonds. So it was all over, no matter what she did.

The important thing was to stay alive. For her own sake, and the sake of the children.

She said, "You won't kill me?"

"Why should we kill you?" It was the same seducer's voice he used, and it made her know he did intend to kill her. But the other one? Would he stand for it if she cooperated, if she pleaded with him, mentioned the children, did whatever they asked?

She said, "Down to the right. The last room on the left. In the closet. There's a pair of overshoes in there."

"In the overshoes?"

She nodded. "In two cloth bags inside the overshoes."

He said to the younger one, "Watch her," and left the room.

She looked at the younger one. Wasn't his face familiar? She felt as though she'd seen him somewhere. At some diplomatic function perhaps, or some social occasion in Tchidanga.

She tried to smile at him, but it didn't work very well. She said, "You don't have to kill me, you know. I won't cause you any trouble."

He didn't say anything, but she thought she detected sympathy in his expression. She said, "I have three children, you know. They're all I care about, not the diamonds or politics or anything else. I wouldn't want to leave them alone, with no one. So you don't have to kill me, you can leave me here, and I promise you I'll never—"

The other one came back in. He nodded to the younger one and patted the pocket of his jacket. "Got them," he said. He turned and looked at Lucille and said, "I'm sorry."

Looking at him, meeting his eye, she realized with a shock that he *was* sorry. It wasn't mockery after all; he was deeply troubled by what he was doing here tonight.

Too late she understood she'd made her appeal to the wrong one.

7

Aaron Marten stood at the window looking out over River-side Drive and the Hudson toward New Jersey. A few lights defined buildings over there even at this hour of the morning.

Jock Daask said, "It's the woman I'm thinking about."

"I'm sure you are," Bob Quilp said.

Marten listened to the voices behind him and looked at the lights across the river.

Jock was saying, "How do we know she isn't in trouble with the police herself? She's traveling with a wanted man; they could be after her, too. And here we are giving her to them."

Still facing New Jersey, Marten said, "Can't be helped. We warned them to stay out of it."

Bob said sarcastically, "You could go on up there tomorrow and untie her if you wanted. Untie her legs, anyway."

Marten did look around then, frowning at Bob. "That will be enough of that," he said.

Bob shrugged, a sardonic smile on his face. "Just trying to be helpful."

Jock came walking across the room toward Marten, a pleading expression on his face. "Aaron," he said, "what difference does it make? Why *can't* we let him live? We'll be in Africa, for heaven's sake. He'll have his woman back. Why kill him?"

Marten shrugged. "I don't want to spend the rest of my life looking over my shoulder for him," he said. "It's as simple as that."

Bob said, "He must have impressed you tonight."

"He did."

Jock said, "Why? Why is it all different now? Why change the plans at all?"

"I don't want him alive," Marten said, and turned his back and looked out at the river again.

Was this the first time in his life he had actively desired the death of another man? Marten thought it was. There had been other moments when the death of this one or that one, known or anonymous, was necessary to the completion of something else that Marten wanted, but this was the first time that the death itself was the goal.

He thought it was Parker's eyes, or perhaps the bone structure of his face. He didn't know what it was exactly, but talking with Parker tonight, listening to his voice, looking at his eyes, watching him move, he understood that Parker was the most dangerous man he had ever met, and that he had made himself Parker's enemy, and that he would not sleep securely at night so long as Parker was still alive. He had had the irrational urge to pull out his pistol and kill Parker right then, almost as a nervous tic, but he had controlled it. *Not until afterwards*, he had thought, *not until we have the diamonds. We need him alive until we have the diamonds.*

But afterwards he must die.

Bob broke the silence behind him at last, saying, "Shouldn't we be on our way?"

Marten turned around again. The clock on the mantel said not quite two fifty. "Not yet," he said. "We don't want to be there too early."

"I don't understand that," Bob said. "We'd do better to be there ahead of them, that's what I say."

Marten shook his head. "We wouldn't. Parker was right about that. If we get there first, we're likely to leave traces when we break in. Then Gonor and the others come along, they see marks on the door or whatever, and they don't come in at all."

Bob shook his head and started to pace around the room.

115

"I don't trust Parker," he said. "I don't like doing things to *his* suggestions."

"Why not?" Marten spread hs hands, saying, "If there's something I'm not seeing, Bob, I'm willing to listen."

Bob made an angry gesture and kept pacing.

"Parker *wants* to tell us the truth," Marten said. "He *wants* us to get the diamonds, because he wants his woman back. After that he may be dangerous, but not before."

"I don't trust him."

"Bob, there's nothing he can do to us. There's no way he can get at us. He doesn't know where the farm is and he doesn't know about this apartment. He can't find his woman without our help and he can't find us."

Jock said doubtfully, watching Bob pace back and forth, "But what if he's guessed we mean to kill him?"

"Then he wouldn't tell us anything. It doesn't do him any good to send us on a wild-goose chase. Say this museum *isn't* where they're taking the diamonds. Say we go there at five o'clock and break in and the place is empty. What good does that do him?"

"He might have warned the police," Bob said. "It could be a trap."

Marten shook his head. "What good does it do him? He wants his woman. If we don't get the diamonds we don't call him; we don't tell him where she is. Believe me, he's sitting in his hotel room right now next to the phone waiting for us to call, hoping we don't lose out to Gonor and his people."

"It makes sense," Bob said grudgingly. "It's smooth and it's easy and it makes sense. But I've just got a feeling."

"I hope you're wrong." Marten told him. "I think you are. I don't think Parker is stupid, and it would be stupid for him to try to double-cross us. We hold all the cards."

Bob shrugged. "I hope you're right," he said.

8

Until he heard the explosions from inside the museum, Gonor sat quietly in the truck smoking his pipe, watching the rare automobile drive by, once watching a police car roll slowly down the block without its occupants appearing to take any interest in the truck, watching the silent and empty street, thinking about the past and the future, thinking about Major Indindu and the future of Dhaba and thinking about the future of himself.

The first explosion, muffled but unmistakable, broke into his calm and reflective mood, making him tense and nervous, and the second explosion made him far too jittery to sit still.

He knew he shouldn't leave the truck. If something went wrong inside the museum, Formutesca and Manado would come out at a dead run expecting him to be in the truck ready to start the engine and get them away from there. But he couldn't help it; he had to move. He had to get out and stand and move and walk around, even if only for a minute or two.

He left the pipe on the dashboard and stepped out on to the sidewalk. The air was damply cold with a chill that went straight to the bone, but he didn't mind. It was too pleasant to stretch his legs, to move around.

He looked at the museum and noticed lights on now on the top floor. There seemed to be no signs of trouble, so he started to walk. He walked up toward Park Avenue halfway to the corner and was about to turn and go back, when he noticed the car parked across the street. Was that paleness in there a white face?

Maybe it was Parker come back after all to be sure things

were going well. But no, it couldn't be. That wasn't the way Parker did things.

So who was it? Someone watching, intending to steal the diamonds once they were brought out of the building?

It was too much of a coincidence, someone's waiting in a car on this block at this hour in the morning. It had to be somebody involved, somebody after the diamonds. Hoskins maybe, or one of Goma's men.

Gonor turned away, acting as though he'd noticed nothing. He walked back toward the truck and then past it and on down to the corner. Then, hurrying, he crossed the street to the right and went down Lexington Avenue to Thirty-seventh Street and so around the block, coming at the car from behind. He moved cautiously on the dark street, his pistol in his hand now held against his side out of sight, and when he reached the car he was surprised to find it empty.

Had he made a mistake before? Had there been no one in the car at all?

He heard a tiny scraping sound behind him and spun, and someone standing there poked a hard finger into his stomach. He saw it was Hoskins, his face distorted with strain, and then the hard finger exploded in his stomach and he never knew anything again.

9

Hoskins stepped back quickly and watched Gonor fall against the side of the car and then crumple and drop to the ground. *So it's going to be bloodshed, is it?* Hoskins thought, as though the decision had belonged to someone else but he had expected it. Waiting around, all this time, but knowing that sooner or later it would have to start.

After Walker had done that strong-arm business the other night, hanging him out the window, Hoskins had decided the time had come to play things a whole lot cagier. There were too many hard cases involved, and if Will Hoskins was going to come out of this with the boodle in hand and his head on his shoulders, it was obvious he was going to have to play a quiet and cautious game.

Quiet and cautious, that's the ticket. Let the hard cases flex their muscles and push each other around. Old Will Hoskins, watching it all from the background, knowing a little bit more than any one of them about what all of them were up to, would know when to move in, when to make that one effective move that would bring him home the bacon and leave the strong-arm boys with egg on their faces.

For himself, Will Hoskins didn't like the hard cases. Brawn instead of brains, violence instead of good planning. He didn't like them, didn't trust them, didn't want to have anything to do with them. He'd avoided them all his life, and if this boodle weren't so damned big he'd have avoided them this time as well.

Particularly after Walker had done that hanging-out-the-window trick. Marten and his playmates had acted rough and mean, but they didn't hold a candle to Walker.

If that was his name, which Hoskins doubted. He was calling himself Lynch this time in town, and that was probably another flag. But whatever he called himself and whatever his real name, Hoskins wanted nothing to do with him. He was just as pleased, he told himself, that Walker *wouldn't* come in with him. He was better off playing a lone hand. He'd played a lone hand before, though never with strong-arm types involved.

Wilfred Hoskins had worked a lot of non-violent rackets in the course of his life, everything from hustling bridge on Long Island to roping for a wire store in Houston. He'd never turned down a chance to wangle a dollar in his life, and when that spade Gonor showed up with his burglary night-school idea, Hoskins immediately saw there was a way in there to promote for himself the sweetest piece of cake of his lifetime. And he still thought so.

He'd been keeping track of Walker since the window episode, keeping well out of Walker's sight but keeping pretty close tabs on him just the same, and when he and Gonor spent almost an hour in that African museum this afternoon he'd told himself it had to mean something. They weren't in that place for fun. When Walker and Gonor split after the museum, it was Walker that Hoskins followed back to his hotel. And then nothing happened for so long that Hoskins was about ready to call it a night, when there was Walker again, coming out of the elevator, coat on, Aaron Marten at his side.

It was nine o'clock. Hoskins watched the two of them, followed them from the hotel, saw them walk a block and a half and then go into a German restaurant on Forty-sixth Street, saw them sit down to dinner together, and then he knew all he needed to know.

First, Walker hadn't wanted to throw in with Hoskins because he'd already thrown in with Marten and that crowd. Birds of a feather, of course. And no doubt Walker, a violent man himself, had been impressed by the tough manner of

Marten and his friends.

But second, the more important, if Walker and Marten were meeting like this it could only mean one thing: that the robbery was set for tonight. And if the robbery was going to be tonight, after Walker and Gonor had spent this afternoon at that museum, then the museum was where the robbery would take place. That had to be where the Kasempa brothers were hiding out.

It all tied together. The only question was, what was Hoskins going to do about it?

In a way, he knew that what he should do about it was nothing. He should clear out of this affair right now; it wasn't where he belonged. Walker, Marten, Gonor, the Kasempas — they were all of them men of violence, and he was a man of reason. And they were all banded into groups; he was the only lone agent. If he were sensible, he'd go straight back to Los Angeles tonight.

But he couldn't do it. There was too much money at stake; it was too great an opportunity. If he could bring it off he'd be on easy street the rest of his life.

He didn't stick around the restaurant once Walker and Marten had settled themselves. He hurried to Sixth Avenue where his rented Ford was waiting in a parking garage, got it out, and drove down to East Thirty-eighth Street. He drove down that block once, slowly, and there were lights in the top-floor windows of the museum. So he'd been right.

He went around the block, came back, and parked near the corner of Park Avenue and on the opposite side of the street from the museum. He cut the engine, adjusted himself comfortably, and waited to see what would happen.

For a long while nothing at all happened, and when the truck parked across the street, in front of the museum, Hoskins at first thought that meant nothing, too. But he kept watching the truck and he saw that it had turned out its lights and there was no more puff of white exhaust at the back, and yet no one had gotten out of it. He didn't understand what

121

that meant, but he was sure it had something to do with Walker and Gonor and the diamonds, and when eventually he saw Gonor's two young partners crawl out of the back of the truck and carry a lot of stuff into the building next door to the museum he'd known his hunch had paid off.

Nothing happened then for a long while until he heard a muffled sound like *thum*. It was more concussion than sound, and if he hadn't had his window open a little to let out the cigarette smoke he wouldn't have heard it at all. He frowned out through the windshield, wondering what it meant or if it had anything to do with the robbery, and then he saw the top floor of the museum starting to light up again, lights first in one window, then in two, then in all. And another *thum*.

Should he move now? Something was happening over there. Should he make his move or should he go on waiting and watching? Move here, or follow the truck and see where the diamonds went next?

Before he'd decided, the curb-side door of the truck opened. He couldn't see it from where he was, but he saw through the window on the near side that the interior light had lit. He waited and watched, and the light went out, meaning the door had shut over there, and a few seconds later he saw Gonor walking on the sidewalk.

Strolling along up toward Park Avenue as though just out for an evening's walk, taking the air, nothing on his mind at all. With those yellow lights gleaming in the top floor of the museum.

Hoskins watched, and he knew when Gonor saw him. He'd hoped it was dark enough in the car here, but Gonor's halted posture was unmistakable. He saw that break in the stride, then saw Gonor try to pick it up again, try to act as though he hadn't seen a thing. But Hoskins was sensitive to nuances where his own safety was concerned, and he knew he'd been seen.

He watched Gonor walk back toward the truck, and he wondered what he should do now. Maybe start the engine,

122

leave the lights off, make a sudden dash for it. Wait till the light down at the corner there had been green for a while, just before it was ready to change.

But Gonor didn't stop at the truck. What was he up to? Hoskins watched him walk all the way down to the corner, then cut across and disappear down Lexington Avenue, and he thought: *Oh-ho, circling my flank.* He got out of the rented car at once and walked up to the side entrance of the church on the corner and stood in the darkness there, and in a little while he saw Gonor walk by and go down and look in the car.

Hoskins followed him, walking directly up behind him, his own gun in his hand, and he didn't plan what he was going to do or think about what he was going to do. He just moved forward. And when Gonor spun around and stared at him it was the most natural thing in the world to push the gun forward and pull the trigger.

So it was all going to work out after all. Gonor was lying on the curb beside the car, so Hoskins rolled him into the gutter and then shoved him part-way under the car where he would be less likely to be seen. Then he went down to the truck, saw that it was indeed empty, and got into it himself. Those other black boys would be getting a surprise when they came out.

But it was a longer wait than he'd anticipated, nearly twenty minutes, and now that he'd actually done something this inactivity was hard to take, which is why he made his error. He saw the museum door open and then shut, he saw the two black figures hurry down the walk and open the gate and start across the sidewalk toward him, and he fired about three seconds too soon.

Not too soon to hit; he shot twice, and the one he'd aimed at flipped backwards and didn't move after he landed. But the other one had time to dive for cover, and the cover of the iron fence was close enough, and he managed to leap over it before Hoskins could get a good bead on him. Hoskins fired anyway, and the shot pinged away in a ricochet.

Damn! Hoskins shoved the truck door open, knowing he

had to get over there and finish that one off before he could get himself organized, and he jumped out on to the sidewalk, took two steps, and a voice called, "Hoskins!"

He turned his head, and to the left along the sidewalk was Parker running toward him. In a panic of haste, Hoskins tried to turn around, or point the gun at Parker, or run away, or keeping going the way he'd been moving, all the contradictory impulses slowing him long enough for Parker to stop running and raise his arm.

Hoskins tried to duck the bullet.

Four

1

Parker was in a bind. He had too much to do and too little time to do it in. And fools like Hoskins didn't help.

Formutesca came out from behind the fence. He looked bewildered. He said, "What happened?"

"That's the question," Parker said. "Where's Gonor?"

"He's supposed to be in the truck."

"Look in the back," Parker said. He himself went down on one knee beside Hoskins. He was dead.

Parker got to his feet and looked up and down the street. Formutesca said, "Not in there."

"Come on," Parker said. There was a car parked across the street and up a ways, and Parker went over there and looked inside, but there was nothing in there. Then Formutesca said, "Underneath," and that was where they found Gonor.

Parker dragged the body on to the sidewalk, and Formutesca said, "Is he hurt bad?"

"He's dead. Take his feet."

"What?"

"Take his feet. We can't leave him out here."

"Oh." Formutesca went down to Gonor's feet, but then said, "He's face down. Shouldn't we turn him over?"

"No," Parker said. He bent and took Gonor under the arms. "Come on, Formutesca."

Formutesca shook his head trying to clear it. "I'm sorry," he said. He lifted Gonor by the ankles. "His feet are skinny," he said.

They crossed the street and went up to the entrance of the museum. Parker held Gonor propped up while Formutesca unlocked the door; then they carried the body in and set it down on the floor. Looking down, Formutesca said, "What a waste. What an awful waste."

"Go move the truck," Parker told him. He had to keep Formutesca moving; he was the only one left who could be used.

Formutesca looked at him vaguely. "Move the truck?"

"Put it down in the next block and then hurry back here. Go on, move."

Formutesca nodded, still vague, but when he went out he did move fast. Parker followed him out, and as Formutesca got into the truck Parker went to the two bodies lying on the sidewalk. He grabbed Hoskins as he'd carried Gonor and dragged him up the walk and into the museum. He left the body beside the other one and hurried back out to take a look at Manado.

The boy was alive but unconscious. He'd been hit twice, once in the left side just above the waist, once high on the left shoulder. It looked as though neither bullet was in him. The lower wound was still bleeding, and his hands were cold.

Parker picked him up in his arms and carried him into the museum. There was a padded bench along the side wall and Parker put him down there. He turned as Formutesca came trotting in.

Parker said, "Shut the door."

Formutesca did, and said, "What now?"

"We'll take Manado upstairs. It'd be best to take the whole bench."

"All right."

The bench was heavy, and it was slow work carrying it with Manado on it the length of the building to the elevator. Once they got it inside and were on their way to the fourth floor, Parker said, "Do you have a doctor you can trust?"

"Major Indindu is a doctor."

Parker was surprised. He said, "Your candidate for president?"

Formutesca smiled. "Yes," he said. "We still need Renaissance men in Africa. Major Indindu is a military man, a politician, a physician and a teacher. He has also worked for a shipping line and been a journalist."

"Call him when we get upstairs," Parker said. "Is the phone still working?"

"Oh, yes. Things went beautifully, just the way you said they would." He shook his head. "In here, I mean."

"Hoskins couldn't keep away," Parker said.

"How did he know to be here?"

They were at the fourth floor. The door slid back. Parker said, "He must have followed somebody."

"What are *you* doing here?"

"Later," Parker said. "We take care of Manado first. Lift."

Formutesca wanted to go on asking questions, but he shrugged and lifted his end of the bench instead. They carried it down the hall and into the first bedroom they reached.

Parker said, "Take a look in the medicine cabinet. We need something to stop the bleeding. Then call Indindu."

"All right."

Formutesca left, and Parker moved Manado from the bench to the room's double bed. He opened Manado's clothing, then stuffed a pillow against the wound in the side. Manado made a small noise in his throat, and his head moved slightly.

Parker looked at his watch. Quarter to four. An hour and fifteen minutes to get everything cleared away and organized.

There were sirens. He went to the window and looked down and saw two police cars come to a stop in the middle of the block. The occupants got out, walked around, looked up at the buildings, looked into the few parked cars, talked to one another. They didn't seem to know what to do. Nobody came out of any of the buildings to tell them anything.

After a minute they got back into their cars and, without sirens, drove away.

2

Major Indindu came into the living-room. "He'll be all right," he said. "He's in shock, of course, and he's lost a lot of blood, but he'll survive."

"Good," Formutesca said. He was obviously too nervous to sit; he'd been pacing back and forth for twenty minutes now. Parker, having made himself a pot of coffee in the kitchen, had been sitting by the window drinking the coffee and watching the street. Nothing had happened since the police had left and Major Indindu had arrived. It was now twenty minutes to five.

The Major said, "Is there more of that coffee?"

"A pot in the kitchen," Parker told him.

"I'll get you some," Formutesca said.

"Thank you."

As Formutesca hurried from the room, the Major walked over to Parker and said, "Frankly, I don't understand where you fit into all this. Things seem to have gotten more confused than poor Gonor indicated to me."

"Gonor did some things wrong at the beginning," Parker said. "They came back to bite him at the end."

The Major looked doubtful. "Was it as simple as that?"

"Yes. He went to Hoskins, he told Hoskins the story without first finding out if Hoskins was the right man, and after that Hoskins couldn't keep away. He'd been told how much gravy there was here and he couldn't help himself; he had to try for it."

"Couldn't you have done anything?"

"I did. I leaned on him. I told him to go away. I hung him out my hotel window."

"You should have dropped him," the Major said.

Parker shook his head. "No. He was an irritation to me, that's all, so I made sure he wouldn't hang around me and bother me. I didn't have to kill him for that, and Gonor didn't hire me to do any killings for him. I told Gonor that Hoskins was hanging around, that he could be trouble. If Gonor had wanted him dead he should have done it himself."

"Did you know Hoskins would try something tonight?"

"No. I thought he'd been convinced."

"Perhaps Gonor did too."

Parker shrugged. "We were wrong."

"You're supposed to be the professional at this," the Major said.

"Not at people. Nobody's a professional at people. Hoskins was a con man, nothing else. He'd never made a direct offensive move in his life. There was no reason to suppose he'd act that way tonight. You can use hindsight and make it make sense, but you couldn't have called it ahead of time. Besides, Gonor was over by Hoskins' car, on the other side of the street, so it looks as though Gonor went to him and forced the issue. Hoskins might have been figuring on just hanging around, watching, following them after they left here, hoping for a time when he could pull a sneak on them."

Formutesca came in with the Major's coffee. "Here you are, sir. Cream, no sugar."

"You remembered. Thank you so much."

Formutesca said to Parker, "You know, I was thinking. It's a good thing you came back. I couldn't have taken charge out there. I'd have fallen apart. I'd have just stood around shaking in my boots till the police showed up."

The Major said, "I'm sure you would have done well, Bara."

Formutesca smiled weakly and shook his head. "I'm sure I wouldn't."

The Major sipped at his coffee, then said to Parker, "How

is it that you *did* appear? I was under the impression you had left for good this afternoon."

"I did. But other things happened."

"For instance?"

"Sit down," Parker told him. "This'll take a while."

3

Parker said:

My woman was supposed to be waiting for me in Boston. When I left Gonor I went to my hotel to check out and take the shuttle flight to Boston. In my room was one of Goma's white troops, one of the three that had tried to muscle me into keeping out of this. He told me he and his friends had taken my woman and they had her in a safe place. When they got the diamonds I could have her back.

I said there wasn't any way I could get the diamonds away from you people by myself, and he said his group would take care of getting them — all I had to do was tell him what was going on tonight, where you people would be, what the plan was.

I told him I wanted to think it over, I needed some time. Mostly I didn't want to tip things too early; I didn't want his bunch breaking in here before you people. So we sat around my room for a while, and then we went and had dinner, and then I gave him a story.

I told him the Kasempas were holed up out on Long Island on a small estate on the north shore. I told him I'd only been out there once — we didn't want to make ourselves conspicuous hanging around, so I was vague about where the place was. I said we worked out our attack plan from a map of the property Gonor had made plus blueprints of the house. I said I thought the house belonged to the UN mission of one of the other African countries near Dhaba, but I didn't know which one.

I said you people were going to hit the place at two this morning, that you were going to kill everybody and then set

133

the place on fire to cover up. I said the place was so isolated nobody would know about the fire until at least tomorrow sometime. And I said that afterwards you weren't going back to Gonor's apartment, you were coming here to this unused museum.

I told him the reason you were coming here was you didn't know if there'd be any casualties or not, you weren't sure what shape you'd be in afterward, and there was this empty apartment on the top floor. That you'd laid in first-aid supplies up here, and fresh clothing, and you were going to stay here overnight and then hide the diamonds somewhere in the museum tomorrow and go on about your business.

He didn't have any clear idea how to go about hijacking you, so I made him some suggestions. I told him it would be too tricky to try anything out at the estate on Long Island, even if he could find it. There was no point going into the middle of somebody else's battle. Also, it wouldn't be a good idea to try anything with you people in your car on the way back. I said in the first place, I didn't know what car you were going to use, and I didn't know what route you were going to use. But even if they did find you on the road somewhere, if they tipped their hand then you might be able to get away from them and then you'd change your plans because you'd know your security was shot, and after that there was no telling where you'd go or what you'd do.

I told him I wanted to help him figure out a good plan because I didn't want him to go up against you people and lose. I wanted my woman back too much for that. That made sense to him, so he listened to me.

I said his best bet would be to come here. I said they shouldn't come before you got here because they'd have to break in, and that would leave marks you people would see. But I was pretty sure you planned to do some drinking when you got back here, and in any case none of you would be alert — you'd be feeling the after-effects of the tension of doing the thing out on Long Island — so the thing for them to do was

134

get here after you'd been here maybe an hour. I told them the front door would be easy to get through, and none of you would hear them because you'd be four floors up.

He thought that should work out, and he told me to go back to my hotel room and wait. Maybe they'd try my idea, maybe not, but one way or the other they'd go for the diamonds tonight, and once they got them they'd give me a call and tell me where to meet them. Then I would go to the place they said, and they'd tell me where to find my woman.

I don't know if she's alive or not. I think there's a chance she is, because they know they don't have anything to be afraid of from her. But I do know they plan to try to kill me. That's the only reason to have me meet them after they get the diamonds. If they were going to tell me where she was and let it go at that they could do it over the phone.

That's why I told them the story I did. And after I left Marten I went to the hotel in case he had anybody following me, and then I got out again and went to his place on Riverside Drive, an address I got from Hoskins a while ago. I wanted to know for sure what Marten would do. I thought Marten was sure he had me mousetrapped, but I didn't want to take any chances.

I went to his place and I saw the other two get there. What I would do if I was Marten at that point, I'd come stake out the museum and wait for you people to show up. Just to be sure Parker wasn't setting me up for something. And if that's what they'd done, I would have had to try to take them alone some way. It would have been early enough, before you people were here.

But Marten must be sure of himself. Or sure of me. Anyway, he stayed there, all three of them stayed there. I waited around as late as I could, wanting to be sure they weren't going anywhere, and then I came over here. I wanted to get here before you left, but I didn't want to butt in till your caper was over, so I waited up by the corner for about fifteen minutes. Then the shooting started and I saw something was wrong, so I came on down.

The reason I came was, I figured you people had gotten me into this situation, you could work with me to get me out of it again. I figured we'd let Marten and the other two break in here, then we'd grab them. You people are good at asking questions; you could ask them where my woman is. After that you could do whatever you wanted with them. Put them down in the basement with the Kasempas. Anything you want.

I didn't figure on the mess Hoskins made. I was counting on Gonor, and we could have used Manado. But the situation's still the same. They're coming here at five o'clock, ten minutes from now. I want you to help me.

4

There was a little silence, and then Major Indindu said without expression, "I see." Standing there in the middle of the room, the saucer held on the palm of his left hand, he finished the last bit of coffee in his cup and said, "Bara, if you would be so kind — another cup?"

Formutesca obviously didn't want to leave the room. He looked at Parker, then at the Major, and reluctantly said, "Of course, sir." He took the cup and saucer and left the room.

The Major said, "Ten minutes, you say. That doesn't leave us much time."

"Enough," Parker said.

"Perhaps. There are a few things I would like to say."

"Go ahead."

"I believe — how can I best phrase this? — I believe you have made some false assumptions."

"Such as?"

The Major looked troubled. "We have to be realists, Mr Parker," he said. "And realistically, we owe you nothing. You were hired to perform a specific task for us. You did so, very well, and you received full payment. We have no more call on you, and you have no more call on us."

"All right," Parker said. "You better take Manado with you."

Surprised, the Major said, "I beg your pardon?"

"They're coming here. In seven minutes. I have to make a try for them; I don't have any choice, and this is the place where I'm doing it. They're going to want the diamonds, so if I lose out to them they'll look around. If they find Manado they may want to wake him up and ask him some questions. So you better take him along."

"Just a moment," the Major said. "You go too fast."

"We have seven minutes. And they could get here early."

"Yes, I understand that. But you didn't take my meaning. I didn't mean you wouldn't be helped." The Major stopped, looking confused. It was clear he was used to a world in which more words did less, where the sentences were long and full and didn't move very far forward. Having to say the whole thing at once was turning out to be difficult.

Parker prompted him. "What did you mean?"

"I simply meant—" The Major made vague hand motions, then gathered himself together and said, "What I meant was that you have no *call* on our services. Only young Formutesca is left to help you, and since you have no call on us I could not *order* him to work with you. But if he is willing to, I certainly would not stand in his way. The morality of the situation, it seems to me, is clearly on the side of—"

"What about you?"

The Major stopped his speech and said, "Me? I don't understand."

"You can stay, too," Parker told him. "That 'major' on your name means you're a military man, doesn't it?"

The Major shook his head in astonishment. "Me? That's out of the question!"

"Why?"

"Mr Parker, if all goes well I will be the next president of Dhaba. I cannot afford to risk myself in a gun battle here; it would be pointless and ridiculous."

Formutesca had come in with the fresh coffee while the Major was speaking.

Parker said, "In other words, you're too valuable."

Formutesca, holding the cup out, said, "Sir?" He was looking slightly confused.

"Thank you." The Major took the cup, then looked levelly

138

at Parker. "If you want to phrase it that way, yes. I am too valuable. I believe Formutesca here will agree with me on that."

Formutesca, looking at the two of them, said, "Too valuable for what?"

The Major said, "Mr Parker wants us to stay here and help him against the three that are coming here. I told him if you wanted to stay it would be your own choice, I couldn't order you to do it. He wanted me to stay as well, and I told him I could not afford to risk myself in such a way. I believe that I am too valuable." He turned to Parker. "To Dhaba, Mr Parker. Not to myself, to Dhaba."

"Of course, sir," said Formutesca. Turning to Parker he said, "The Major is the only hope we have, Mr Parker. If anything happens to him, there won't be anyone to stop Goma. Colonel Lubudi can't last long, not now, and if the Major isn't there to step in and take his place, General Goma will walk right in and take over the country."

Parker said, "A General. A Colonel. A Major."

With a thin smile, the Major said, "Do you mean we're all alike, Mr Parker?"

"I don't know anything about your politics," Parker told him. "Or anybody's politics. It's four minutes to five. Formutesca, I could use you. If you want to stay."

"Well, sure," Formutesca said. "Naturally."

"Good," Parker said. "Major, you'd better get out of here. You have a car out front?"

"Yes."

"Formutesca, help him move Manado."

The Major said, "Is it necessary? It would be better—"

"We might lose," Parker said. "Leave him here if you want."

"No." The Major looked more and more troubled.

Parker turned back to Formutesca. "Where are the bodies?"

"In the basement. We just stacked them there, and some things that got bloodied. We were going to come back tomorrow night and bury them."

"They had guns?"

"They're down there, too."

"All right. You people use the elevator, I'll use the stairs. Formutesca, when you're done helping the Major I'll be on the first floor. Leave the lights on up here."

Formutesca nodded. "I will."

Parker headed for the door, but the Major said, "Mr Parker."

He turned. "What?"

The Major was having trouble compressing his thoughts again. "I—" he said, then shook his head and started again. "I do appreciate, I understand your position. I sympathize with your position. I want you to know if there weren't so many other factors to consider, I would—"

"That's good," Parker said. "It's three minutes to five."

He left the room.

5

Parker looked at the armaments on the display case. The ground-floor lights were off, but illumination came in the barred windows from a streetlight just out front. To Parker's right, through an archway, was the main entrance foyer, with a long rectangle of white light on the floor from the open doorway. The display case contained knives and axes, mostly of stone. On the glass top Parker had put all the guns he'd found downstairs: six pistols, two machine guns, one shotgun with the barrels sawed off back to the stock. Parker looked at them and then looked at his watch. Five o'clock. Formutesca was still outside with the Major.

Were Marten and the others on the scene? It wouldn't change anything in their minds for them to see the Major and Formutesca carry Manado out of the building. They could incorporate that into the story Parker had given them with no trouble: Manado must have been wounded during the battle on Long Island, too seriously to be left in the museum. With the fourth-floor lights burning, that must mean Gonor was still upstairs.

The only problem was, would they jump the gun? Would they decide to go for Formutesca out there on the street? They shouldn't; they should prefer to keep things quiet outside and make their move in the privacy of the museum. Also, if they attacked now they would have to believe that Gonor would be alerted to their presence, and it would be better for them to get into the building undetected.

Still, Formutesca was taking a long time. Parker was about to go out after him, when a shadow lined out on the rectangle of light in the foyer, and a second later Formutesca came into sight, peering around into the darkness.

Parker called, "In here. Shut the door."

"Oh! Right."

The rectangle disappeared, and in greater darkness Formutesca came in and stood beside Parker. The weapons on the display case glinted in the patch of light from the streetlight.

Formutesca said, "The Major feels bad, you know. He's afraid you don't understand the—"

"It doesn't matter to me," Parker said. "Where can we stash some of these under lock and key?"

"There's a closet—"

"Good. Put them away, all but those two pistols. I checked; they're both loaded."

Formutesca touched one of the machine guns. "You don't want to use these? Or that shotgun? At close range you can—"

"I want at least one of them alive. I want to shoot to wound, not kill. For that we can't use those things."

"All right." Formutesca filled his pockets with pistols, picked up the machine guns and the shotgun, and carried them away.

Parker went over to the window. It was the deadest part of night: no traffic, no pedestrians. Down to the left at Lexington Avenue a brightly lighted bus rolled slowly by, nobody in it but the driver. Up to the right and across the street was Hoskins' car, its key now in Parker's pocket. Hoskins himself was with Gonor and the Kasempas in the basement.

It was going to be tough for the Major and his people to keep this thing hushed up now, with Gonor dead. The others could have disappeared with nobody to notice — particularly once Colonel Lubudi was no longer president — but Gonor was a known official; his absence would have to be accounted for somehow.

142

Well, that wasn't Parker's problem. The Major would do it, or he wouldn't do it.

Formutesca came back. "Done," he said.

From the window, Parker said, "There's a gun for you on the case there. Take it and go into the room on the other side of the entrance. Wait till they're all the way in before you start to shoot and then aim low. Aim for the legs; we want them alive. And remember I'm over here, so wait till they're a little past you and you can shoot at an angle. I don't want one of your bullets coming over here and getting me."

Formutesca was regaining some of his natural manner. "I don't want it either," he said. "I don't want to be alone in here with that bunch. If they show up. What time is it?"

"They've shown up," Parker said. "Get on over there."

Formutesca, looking startled, ran from the room and across the foyer as Parker looked out the window at the three men coming up the walk.

6

They took a long time getting through the door, and they were very slow and very loud. Parker was about ready to go over and open it for them, when at last they did pop it and come in.

Now they turned pro. They moved well, taking their time, not moving in very far until the door was shut and the foyer back in darkness. Then they went in quick dashes, bent low, almost silent. It implied military training at some time or other.

It also made it difficult to see them and hit them. Parker, against the wall beside the doorway, felt around till he got the light switch for the room he was in and switched it on.

The three of them were bunched at the doorway at the back of the foyer. No direct light from Parker's room reached them, but enough indirect spillage touched them to do the job. Parker fired at their legs, and a second later he heard a shot from Formutesca on the other side.

One of them went down, falling straight down as though the floor had been yanked out from under him. A second recoiled against the wall, white-faced, his arms shooting up in surrender. The third spun around, ducked low, and ran for the door.

Parker snapped off a quick shot at the running one, but missed. He came out into the light, but then he couldn't shoot because Formutesca had come out too and was directly across the way. They stared across at one another in a frozen second that seemed to go on for years.

The running man reached the door, slammed it open, and leaped the front steps, landing on all fours on the walk. He was up like a sprinter, hurdled the wrought-iron fence, and was away down the street to the left.

Parker ran out the front door and saw him jump into a car down there. It was too late to do anything about it. He turned and went back into the museum, shutting the door after him. He switched on the foyer light. The one with his hands up was still standing there, round-eyed, terrified, looking sixteen years old. He had a huge automatic in his right hand shaking up there above his head. He'd obviously forgotten he was holding it.

The other one was doubled on the floor clutching his left thigh. Over and over he was saying, "Jock. Help me, Jock."

Neither one was Marten. Marten was the one who'd gotten away.

Parker went over to the standing one. "You're Jock?"

A spastic nod.

"You're holding a gun, Jock. Open your hand and let it drop."

Jock abruptly looked twice as terrified as before. He opened his hand, making a little pushing movement, and the automatic fell in an arc. Parker caught it in his free hand and put it in his hip pocket.

These were the other two who'd been with Marten back at the beginning when they'd tried to muscle him out of working for Gonor. Jock here had been the phlegmatic one by the door. The other one, now lying on the floor, had been the one who had shown the hardware that first time.

Parker said, "Jock, I want some fast answers. Is she still alive?"

"Yes!" the word was shouted as much in surprise as anything else. Jock stared at Parker with astonishment now mixed with the fear. "What do you think we are?"

"Where is she?"

The one on the floor said, "Keep your trap shut, Jock. Don't tell him a goddam thing."

Jock looked from Parker to the one on the floor and back to

145

Parker. His mouth was open but he wasn't saying anything.

Parker said, "Formutesca, take that one to the cellar."

Formutesca said, "Kill him?"

"Up to you. Jock, if you want to live through this you'll tell me where she is."

Formutesca was dragging the other one across the floor, neither of them making a sound. Jock, staring at them, said, "You can't do that. You can't just drag him away and murder him; you can't do it."

Parker said to Formutesca, "Hold it." To Jock he said, "We'll leave him there. You take me to where she's being kept; then you can come back here and take care of him."

The one on the floor cried, "Don't tell him, Jock! Aaron can still make another try for the diamonds."

Everybody looked at him. Jock, in bewilderment, said, "Why can't he go for the diamonds anyway? What difference if we tell where the woman is?"

Parker said, "Is that where he's going? Not the apartment on Riverside Drive?"

Jock blinked, staring now at Parker. "You know about the apartment?"

Parker put his hand on Jock's shoulder. "Where is she, Jock?"

7

"You turn left," Jock said. "You see where that big tree is up there? Just past it."

They were in Connecticut. They'd crossed the state line from New York a little north of Brewster, and the last sign they'd seen had pointed toward East Lake off to the right. It was six thirty in the morning now, with vague daylight edging up over the mountains straight ahead.

Parker was at the wheel of Hoskins' rented car with Jock beside him. Formutesca was in the back seat, a pistol at Jock's head. Beside Formutesca were the machine guns and the shotgun. The closet where they'd been stored back at the museum now held Jock's wounded friend.

The tree was an elm, old and thick-trunked and broad, its bare branches looking in the headlights as though they were knotted together. Parker slowed the car, saw the dirt road just past the tree, and made the turn. Accelerating again, the car jouncing on the packed earth, he said, "How much farther to the house?"

"About two miles," Jock said. "We have to go up over a hill. There's a woods."

"In the daytime I wouldn't be able to see the house from here?" What Parker meant was, *Can Marten see my headlights if he's here?*

Jock said, "Oh, no. The hill's in the way; it's the other side of the hill. There's a lake there, past the house. The road goes down to the house and then makes a left and follows the lake for a ways and then stops."

There had been cleared land on both sides when they'd first entered this road, but now they were moving into woods. The road began to twist back and forth as though originally it had been made by somebody who hadn't wanted to chop down many trees.

Parker hunched over the wheel, pushing the car as hard as he could, not knowing whether Marten was out in front of him or not. Jock seemed to think that Marten would lie low in the city, but the other one seemed to be sure that Marten would come up here. Why? To kill Claire, or ambush Parker, or both? The other one had refused to say any more, and there hadn't been time to force answers out of him. Marten had started with about a ten-minute lead, and though Parker had pushed hard all the way up — doing ninety and ninety-five on the Saw Mill River Parkway on the assumption that even state troopers don't like to be out at five or six o'clock of a cold, damp March morning — he had to take it for granted that Marten had done the same, if he was coming this way.

Jock had said Marten was driving a two-year-old Ford Mustang, and Hoskins had rented himself a current model Ford Falcon, so in simple terms of automobile Marten had himself a slight edge. It all depended on which was the better driver. Parker had overtaken no Mustangs along the way, so Marten was either back in the city or still out in front of him.

Parker wasn't sure what Marten might do. He was an arrogant man who would be enraged at Parker having conned him, but he was also a cautious man. It was unlikely he'd come up all this way just to kill Claire, but he might think it worth the effort to rid himself of Parker.

The road was beginning to climb. This must be the hill Jock had mentioned. Parker's foot jabbed back and forth at accelerator and brake as he slued around the curves, lunged up the brief straightaways, and skidded past the trees. Clenching the wheel, staring straight ahead through the windshield, he said, "Let me know when we're almost to the top."

"Yes, sir," said Jock, and the windshield starred in the middle, just under the rearview mirror, and Jock said, "Oh!"

148

He fell sideways, his head hitting Parker's right arm and then landing in his lap.

They were in the middle of a curve. Parker spun the wheel hard, slammed his left foot on the brake, and cut the lights and the ignition. He heard Formutesca make a sudden sound. Jock's limp body came rolling into him more because of the tight turn they were in, and the rear tires scraped and gouged sideways across the dirt and the roadside weeds. Parker couldn't move with Jock all over him, and he kept trying to push the body away.

The left rear of the car hit something, and they jolted to a stop. Parker shoved Jock hard and called to Formutesca, "Out of the car!" At the same time, he leaned over the back seat for the guns.

Formutesca was lying on them. Either he'd been hit by another bullet or he'd knocked himself out when Parker slammed on the brakes. In any case, he was out of the action. Parker pulled him out of the way, and he rolled on to the floor. Parker grabbed a gun butt, pushed open the door, and dove out of the car. The interior light had gone on when he'd opened the door — there hadn't been anything he could do about that — and he heard the sound of two quick shots as he leaped into the darkness at the side of the road.

He rolled, came up against a tree trunk, and scrambled around to the other side of it. The car door was still open, lighting the center of the stage. When he stopped there was no longer any sound.

It was the shotgun he'd grabbed. Disgusted, he almost threw it away, but changed his mind and kept it. Holding it in his left hand, he took out his pistol and waited behind the tree for whatever would happen next.

It had been impossible to tell where the last two shots had come from. He'd been in motion himself at the time they were fired, and they could have come from any direction at all. The first shot, having hit the middle of the windshield and then the person on the right side of the front seat, must

149

have been fired from in front and off the road to the left, but that had been while they were in the middle of a curve. The car had slued farther around the curve after the shot, and by now that guide to Marten's direction was almost useless. The only thing that could be said for sure, since the curve was to the right, was that Marten had to be on this side of the road.

Dawn was coming. Here in the woods on the hillside it was still pitch black night, but Parker remembered the vague paleness against the mountains in the eastern sky. In half an hour, maybe forty-five minutes, it would be possible to see in here.

The question was, should he wait or not? The alternative was to try to get past Marten and on over the hill and down to the farmhouse. Marten himself might try that, preferring to be safely hidden indoors when daylight came. But it would be impossible to get to the farmhouse in the dark without sticking to the road, which could be dangerous.

If Marten would make a noise, any kind of noise, it would help. But he was silent; the woods were silent. Far away Parker could faintly hear birds starting to announce morning to each other, but the gunfire in this part of the woods had silenced everything.

Could he draw Marten's fire? Parker felt around on the ground, picked up a small stone, and tossed it in the direction away from the road and the car. It fell into a bush with a faint rustling noise.

Nothing.

Parker waited, watching and listening. No response.

He didn't dare wait for daylight. Marten could be on his way to the farmhouse now. Aside from Claire, there was the problem of letting Marten get set inside the house.

Parker moved. He inched around the tree and moved away at a diagonal away from the lit automobile in the road. When he could barely see the light through the trees he angled back toward the road again. He moved silently, the pistol in his right hand and the shotgun in his left, going in quick spurts

150

from tree to tree, stopping and listening, hearing nothing, moving on.

He reached the road and crossed it in three running leaps. He progressed again on the other side, going uphill now, keeping the light from the car just barely in sight. He knew the road curved over there, and he curved too, planning to come back to it far enough along so he wouldn't be silhouetted on it in the light from the car.

It was black here, totally black. He could see only objects between himself and the car; otherwise he had to move by feel. He'd put the pistol away now and was holding the shotgun down along his left side so it wouldn't bump into anything and make noise. He moved along with his right hand out in front of him guiding him along among the tree-trunks.

He knew he'd reached the road again when his hand found no tree. He stood where he was a minute, the dim light from the car down to his left and behind him, and listened to the silence of the woods. The bird sounds were closer now but still not in this immediate area. Parker turned right and began moving cautiously along the road.

He bumped into the car, not seeing it. He felt his way around to the left side, but the window was rolled up and if he opened the door the interior light would go on.

This had to be Marten's Ford Mustang. Parker would have preferred to put the car out of commission some way, but he had no knife with him and so had no silent way to do it. He felt his way on past the car and continued on down the road.

He'd gone three steps, when he was suddenly bathed in light. He spun around in the glare of four headlights, hearing the Mustang's engine kicking into life.

Marten had gone back to his car. He'd been waiting there, probably for daylight, figuring that inside the car was the one place Parker wouldn't expect to find him. He'd known that sooner or later Parker would have to come up this road.

Parker reacted at once, almost without thinking. The

151

lights flashed on, he spun and saw them, he heard the engine turning over, and he raised the shotgun and fired. The right barrel. The left barrel.

The lights went out.

8

There was no one in the Falcon, though the door was still open and the light still on. Parker walked deliberately within range of that light and called softly, "Formutesca."

"Here."

Formutesca came grinning from the woods at the roadside. "I heard you blast away up there," he said. "Then I heard the pistol shot, so I didn't know who was the winner."

"The pistol shot was me too," Parker said. Marten had been wounded by the shotgun blast but not killed, and Parker had had to finish him at close range with the pistol.

Formutesca said, "So what now?"

"We go to the house. Where's Jock?"

Formutesca jabbed a thumb over his shoulder at the woods. "In there. He's dead."

Parker didn't ask if Jock had died from Marten's shot or from something else. He just nodded and said, "Get in. We'll drive on up to he house."

"Fine."

There was a faint paleness in the air now. Day was beginning, hesitantly. Parker and Formutesca got into the Falcon and Parker started the engine. The car seemed none the worse for wear, except for the starred hole in the windshield and a new dent in the left rear fender. Parker switched on the lights and they drove on up to the Mustang. Parker stopped the Falcon.

He said, "You bring this car down. Get rid of Marten first. Put him in the woods where he can't be seen from the road."

"Right."

They got out of the car and walked up to the Mustang.

Parker got behind the wheel, and Formutesca opened the passenger door and dragged Marten out. He shut the door again and Parker started the engine.

The Mustang would still run. Its headlights were smashed and both front tires were flat, its windshield was mostly gone and there were bloodstains on the black leatherette of the bucket seats, but it would run. Parker put it in gear and drove it slowly on up the hill.

The car didn't want to go. The flat front tires made it buck from side to side of the road, and Parker had to hold the wheel by force to keep the Mustang moving forward. But it did move and took him over the top of the hill and down the other side, and now ahead of him he could see the rambling structure of the house and beyond it the lake.

Gray-white mist lay over the lake. The sun hadn't cleared the mountain ridges to the east yet, but the sky was increasingly gray, and a bleak gray light lay on the world. The trees around the lake looked like dead black skeletons, and the water looked as cold as an underground river.

Parker drove the Mustang off the road and over the shabby lawn to the side of the house. He left it there and went into the house and began to search from room to room.

He found her locked in a bedroom upstairs, lying on her side on the bed tied hand and foot and with a gag in her mouth. He couldn't see her wrists, but her ankles looked raw and burned from the ropes. Her face looked puffy, the eyes closed, and at first he thought she was dead, but then he saw she was asleep.

He heard Formutesca bring the Falcon to a stop out in front of the house. He walked across the room and put a hand on Claire's cheek.

Richard Stark is one of four pseudonyms of Donald Westlake (1933–2008), prolific author of noir crime fiction. Stark's short crime novels about an independent, hardworking criminal named Parker start with *The Hunter* (made into the film *Point Blank*) and end with *Butcher's Moon* (1974)—and then, after more than twenty years, revive with *Comeback* (1998), *Backflash* (1999), and six more, up to the latest, *Dirty Money* (2008). In 1993 the Mystery Writers of America bestowed the society's highest honor on Westlake, naming him a Grand Master. *Comeback* and *Backflash* were selected as *New York Times Notable Books of the Year*. In 2009, *The Hunter* was made into a graphic novel by Darwyn Cooke.